PRAISE FOR
Love and Other Monsters in the Dark

"K.B. Jensen's newest book, *Love and Other Monsters in the Dark,* is a delicious, delightful, chilling thrill ride of a story collection. On full display in these pages are Jensen's sense of the weird and the uncanny and her unsentimental, though wholly accurate view of the human condition. Here, you'll find zombies and bank robbers; a woman who dreams of Alex Trebec; poison where you least expect it; murder, mystery and mayhem. These stories, some only a few paragraphs in length, are deft, sprinkled with dark humor and brilliantly crafted dialogue. I came away from this collection in awe of Jensen's story-telling chops and sheer imaginative prowess. Highly recommended."
—Kathy Fish, award-winning author
of *Wild Life: Collected Works*

"The entries of K. B. Jensen's entertaining flash fiction collection *Love and Other Monsters in the Dark* brim with aching surprises; they feature eccentric secrets and solitary monsters. Whether they are plausible, hyperbolic, or fantastical, these stories relish in circumstances that lead people toward new awareness . . . Jensen's characters are roundly intriguing. They are often both odd and vulnerable, and they are humanized even in weird situations . . . The book's monsters are also diverse and complex, too, from those whose hideousness is physical to those who look like people, but whose souls are corrupt, raising intriguing questions about the forms that darkness takes."
—*Foreword Clarion Review*

K.B. JENSEN

LOVE

AND OTHER Monsters IN THE Dark

· short stories ·

Love and Other Monsters in the Dark: Short Stories
Published by Crimson Cloud Media LLC.
Denver, CO

Publisher's Cataloging-in-Publication data

Names: Jensen, K. B., author.
Title: Love and other monsters in the dark : short stories / K. B. Jensen.
Description: Denver, CO: Crimson Cloud Media LLC, 2022
Identifiers: ISBN: 979-8-9853350-0-2 (paperback) | 979-8-9853350-1-9 (ebook)
Subjects: LCSH Love--Fiction. | Supernatural--Fiction. | Horror fiction. | Noir fiction. | Short stories, American. | BISAC FICTION / Short Stories (single author)
Classification: LCC PS3610.E5662 L68 2022 | DDC 813.6--dc23

Cover by Shira Lee Designs.
Interior design by Victoria Wolf.
Copyright owned by K.B. Jensen

CONTENTS

A Siren in Stone

IN THE MORNING, I heard the woman's soft cries seeping from the stone walls of the 17th-century villa I had booked in Italy. It was my first trip alone after my breakdown. The sobbing echoed. I called out, are you okay? The voice went silent, and I was afraid. There was nothing on the other side.

In the afternoon, I heard the woman's voice again. Jabbering in a language I couldn't understand. I called out, are you okay? And the voice went silent. A soul trapped in stone. *Could she hear me?*

In the evening, I did not hear the woman's voice at all. Heavy rain rattling the roof punctuated the silence. *Was she afraid? Where did she go?* Unheard, unseen, I touched the rough pale white walls, cold against my fingertips. *If only we could escape this darkness together.*

In the night, I heard her laughing. I couldn't sleep. "Leave me alone," I said. High-pitched chit-chattering started. I wondered if it was the rustling of mice. Knew it wasn't. "You sound crazy," I said. "Am I breaking down again?" Was I talking to her or myself? *I have to stop this.*

In the morning, I found a screwdriver and a mallet in a kitchen drawer and started chiseling at the stone. Tap, tap, tap. I heard her shrieking hysterically, as pieces fell. "Don't worry," I whispered. "I'll get you out of this."

In the afternoon, I saw glimpses of the yellow bones in the wall. A femur emerged first, then a delicately curved tibia from the excavation. I was covered in dust with bits of stone grit in between my teeth.

In the evening, the bones were piled next to me on the floor. I pried and dislodged the skull from the stone and peered into her empty eye sockets. "Who are you?" She said nothing. I started the assembly, bleached the bones in boiling water and used bits of thread to tie her together as perfectly as possible.

In the night, I dreamt of gelatinous cold flesh, and organs as malleable as clay in my hands. Her heart was slippery. When I woke, I found I had added the organs and flesh to the bones. I got up and sat her by the radiator to heat up her limp body.

In the morning, I painted her face with a makeup brush, her eyes, eyebrows, and used lipstick to create a soft, red mouth. I propped her up against what was left of the wall, wiped the sweat off her damp forehead, gently pushed her shoulders back and upright. She smiled, mouth agape. Missing a tooth, far from perfect, but free.

Pushing Buttons

"WHO WAS HERE?" he asked.

It started within minutes of him coming home from work. Like he always does, he had washed his hands and thrown a paper towel in the trash can. As the lid opened, his eyes darted to the empty disposable coffee cup at the top of the trash. It was a size medium. I never order a medium. It toppled over.

"Who was here?" he asked again. He was still wearing his suit from work. Hadn't even had a chance to take off the jacket. And it was hot in the kitchen, a real-life cliché.

"What do you mean?" I asked, raising an eyebrow. I was playing the part of innocent housewife in that moment, struck a pose with a hand on a hip. If I had had an apron, I would have worn it. The dishes were not done before he came home either. He hated that. The pot was still half full of noodles on the stovetop, leftover from making the boys lunch to take to school. I never notice these things until he does. He's called me absent minded, but it wasn't that my head was empty. It was that it was too full.

Even now I could read that frown.

"I can tell when someone's been in this house," he said. "I'm observant."

His eyes narrowed, but not in an angry way, necessarily. It was a more discerning look, like he was trying to focus and see things that couldn't be seen.

"I had a friend over in the afternoon," I said flatly.

Was I lying? I saw the question flicker in his eyes, and it told me how little he trusted me.

"It was Kate."

"Kate," he said. An uncertain smile flashed across his face. Was that relief?

I was wearing a new summer dress. But he never noticed that. So much for being observant. He didn't notice my crimson lipstick either. I wondered what the point was of wearing it. I liked the color, but a reaction might have been nice too. Any kind of reaction.

"What if it had been someone else?" I asked. "What would you have done then?"

"I don't know," he said.

"I hate it when you answer my questions that way. When I ask what's bothering you and you say, 'I don't know.'"

"I don't know," he said.

"Would you have taken the knife from the drawer and slit my throat?" I stood up on tippy toes and kissed his cheek, leaving a crimson mark on his face.

"Of course not," he said, turning away. "You *are* the mother of my children." The words cut me instead.

He walked out of the room and shut the door behind him. I could hear him greeting the boys in a warm, deep voice. "The monster's gonna hug you!" he said with a growl.

I went back to the soapy sink full of dishes and my thoughts. He knows me so well, and so little.

If he had been so damn observant, he would have noticed the stain on the edge of the cup. It was the same crimson color as the lipstick I was wearing. Yes, I had lied about Kate.

People change, you know. Just for once, I had ordered a medium.

Killer Blossoms

AN EXTREMELY RARE AND LATE BLOOMER, the Palm of Casper is one of the most dangerous plants in the world if ingested. Experts say a single milligram of its beautiful, ivory blossoms is enough to kill five men. It's the last flower you'd expect to find in an assortment of edible flowers on top of a wedding cake. The bride and groom certainly had no idea. Its poison was rarely tested for in toxicology reports by medical examiners, and its effects mimic severe food poisoning and can cause paralysis.

When Henry nestled the narrow, vase-like flower among the other blossoms, he made sure to squeeze the petals to release more poisonous secretions into the buttercream. The almost translucent milky substance wept from the petals onto the frosting, running down Henry's pointer finger.

Henry had never killed before. His father had died and left everything to his half-sister, not him. If she and her husband died, Henry wouldn't have to worry about his various expenses: too numerous to list here. He couldn't remember ever loving his sister, maybe for a split second before he knew her?

Henry was one of those kids who started speaking later in childhood. At age four, he would only say a word or two if pressed, motioning with his hands. Then seven-year-old Marsha officially joined his family. The first thing Marsha did was decapitate all eight of his GI Joes. When Henry had shown his father the victims and pointed at Marsha. She shrugged and told their father she was pretending to be a surgeon like him, and he had smiled and tousled her curly blond hair with his hand. The heads were never found, though the worst part was Henry spent weeks searching. He had gone through the garbage and even unscrewed all the air ducts in the house, shining a flashlight into the dusty darkness. Even if they had been found, she had used a small saw from the garage, so no subsequent operating could save them.

After weeks of looking, with Marsha watching with crossed arms and endless smirks, Henry had screamed a torrent of cuss words at her in a long sentence that astounded his father. He had always been able to talk but just hadn't wanted to. Henry later excelled in school, a late bloomer, much like the Palm of Casper flower. Some called him good looking, despite a few mild physical defects, an unevenness. After years of Marsha whispering, calling him names—four eyes, dork, and idiot, he switched from glasses to contacts.

Watching his older sister get married, listening to her poor husband profess his undying love. Henry tuned out the vows and remembered his father's last words to him. Dying of cancer, he actually asked Henry, "Why can't you be more like your sister? Smart like her."

Marsha grew up to become a cold and calculating surgeon, with the stomach to slice into living bodies with precision. Fearless, because she didn't care whether they died.

And maybe he was a little like her, after all.

Henry had never been married before, and he hadn't been to a wedding since his father married his stepmother. If he had, he'd know that the small top of the cake is commonly saved for the one-year anniversary, not the cake cutting. The Palm of Casper blossom, even long frozen in Tupperware in a refrigerator, wouldn't lose much potency. In fact, this plan might have even been better to diffuse suspicion, assuming the couple made it through their first year together. Could Marsha hide her true nature that long?

He thought about all these things as he lay in bed that night after the wedding, still in his suit jacket and pants, staring blankly at the ceiling. Paralyzed.

Because you see, funny thing, it doesn't matter how many times you wash your hands. The Palm of Casper secretions are much like those of the ghost pepper, but without the signature sting. The oils leave residue on your hands if you handle them without gloves. And when Henry had taken out his contacts that night, his finger had introduced the poison into his tear ducts.

Edward Shuttleburger Steals an Armadillo on His Day Off

EDWARD SHUTTLEBURGER did not mean to stop taking his medication. For fifteen years, since his diagnosis, he had always taken his pills as prescribed. But one day he opened his pillbox and was startled by a stray cat wandering into his room. He tripped on Fluffy, and the purple pillbox went flying. When they hit the bathroom counter, the pills leapt from the box and scattered into the toilet. Plop. Plop. Plop. Traveling through Europe meant it was difficult to call his psychiatrist.

Ed did not immediately feel the effects of withdrawal or symptoms per se, but felt an intense need to be with someone, anyone. He couldn't bear to be alone. Too afraid of loneliness. Several times, Ed tried calling the psychiatrist, but with the time change got no answer or call back. He knew what would make it better. An armadillo, of course.

He had a brochure for the zoo in Rome. There was a picture of an armadillo on the front of it. Arnie the Armadillo stared at him with sad, beady eyes, while chewing on a tangerine peel. Coincidentally, Edward had been fond of armadillos since he was a child reading his favorite picture book about animals and the alphabet. A for armadillo. He wanted to be an armadillo, to have some kind of armor against the world.

Edward wondered if Arnie had ever had a day off in his life, from the onslaught of tourists staring him down. Or if he just sat there chewing his tangerines, happily. Was Arnie as sedated as he was? Drugged and drowsy from meds? Was Arnie hanging on to normalcy by a thread? He had to save this beautiful creature.

Breaking into the zoo was easy enough. He bought a ticket. Walked in. And found Arnie's enclosure. Was the armadillo the national animal, he wondered? If not, why not? The armadillo was a majestic creature. He hopped the small wooden fence, dust billowed around his shoes, and he reached for Arnie. "Come with me and be free," he said softly, hoping not to draw too much attention.

He reached for the animal and was surprised by how heavy it was. When Arnie bit him, it hurt too. Could an armadillo bite kill you? Edward thought it was an okay way to die. He was fine with it if the armadillo didn't mind.

Final Jeopardy

I HAD A KINKY SEX DREAM about Alex Trebek. It wasn't all bad, but then again, I can remember only snippets of it. Running my fingers through his gray hair. I answered him, "What is the meaning of life?" And he declared me the winner.

I cannot tell you the things he did to me, not without blushing. Then I woke up alone. I felt the need to change the sheets. Sweaty. Stale. I ripped them off and crumpled them in a pile at the foot of the bed. The curtain fluttered open, and the breeze kissed my naked skin.

It's been five years since my husband died. I am not quite ready to be an old woman, not ready to lose myself to grief. I am not lost without him, but I'm not particularly happy either. Perhaps I've been watching too much "Jeopardy." Or maybe I need more of Alex in real life. No one ever talks about the stuff you miss behind closed doors. It's not that I haven't had other men flit in and out of my life since he died. It's just Gregory, my husband, had certain talents that other men just don't have.

I don my robe and fetch the newspaper, a relic of my youth. The thin paper is spread across my kitchen table and anchored with my coffee cup. I read about murder, mayhem, and political scandals and the ink blotches the skin on my hands. It would be interesting if it weren't for the fact that the news seems to repeat each day.

The neighbor walks out on his front porch to get his paper. We might be the last two newspaper subscribers left in the world. They will pry my newspaper from my cold, dead hands, I laugh.

A lot of people die within six months of their spouse departing this world. Grief takes a toll. It's in my chest and my lungs. Parts of me have turned to ash. I threw handfuls of dirt onto Gregory's coffin. It was like I was burying him in pieces of me.

I get up to get myself a second cup of coffee and trip on the rope that's supposed to tie my robe closed. I slip forward. I'm not fast enough to reach out with both hands. I hit my head on the wall on the way down and hear a crack. Was it the wall or my skull?

For a second I see stars, and not in a good way, not the way Alex had me seeing them. And I have a moment of panic. I cannot die today, not mostly naked on a linoleum floor. The air hums in my ears.

I hear Gregory's voice. "Wake up, my darling. Wake up."

I open my eyes, and there he is in our bed, smiling at me. We are young again. He's wearing boxers, and I touch his warm chest, shocked to feel the familiar skin.

"I thought you were gone," I say.

"Time for work," he says. "Silly, groggy honey."

In that moment, I wonder, maybe I am dead and don't even know it. Like I never noticed my own life slip away. And maybe Gregory is dead, and he doesn't know it.

Because like the news spread across my kitchen table, we repeat each day. We use the same words even.

"I love you. Have a good day at work," I say.
And this is it. There is no dollar amount for this answer.

Dark Angels

I WONDERED WHAT IT WAS LIKE to go from cancer to this. At first, I thought it was a mistake when I saw his photos online. In one image, he was gaunt and pale, with hollows under his cheekbones. He embraced his two sons with frail, stick-like arms. In the next photo, he had black metallic wings. He was swooping down from the side of a cliff, his chiseled abdominal and chest muscles rippling beast-like as he soared down. His thick, brown hair blew back with the wind.

In the comments, one of his friends wrote, "He had to work up to that jump with a lot of small ones. Not like he just dove down the cliff on his first try."

Robin had been dying of stomach cancer. But that didn't matter to Uncle Sam. In these times of human engineering, it doesn't matter if you are a man or woman, if you are old or young, disabled or fit, Uncle Sam wants you. Uncle Sam desperately wants you for experiments, for new, cutting-edge human weaponry, to be the perfect, bioengineered soldier. But no one wants to join.

I called Robin when I saw the photo. It had been years since I talked to him, since college actually. The phone rang and rang. He finally picked up. I could hear him breathing heavily on the phone. I could hear click, click noises on the line, like it was a bad connection. But it wasn't a bad connection. It was his claws against the receiver.

"I didn't know you signed up, Rob," I said. "Congratulations. I'm so glad you are alive. I'm sure the kids are so happy.

"What's it like? Can I write about it? I'd love to tell your story. I'm so glad you are alive, man."

Robin told me to come visit the base and have a beer with him. "I'll tell you everything, well, almost everything, but promise you won't make any wisecracks about my name. It's getting old."

I stifled a laugh and made the promise.

I decided to fly out to see him and drive a rental car to Virginia. It would make a good story. I'd never seen a military base covered in wire mesh before, including all sides and above. It looked like one of those old zoo exhibits, before they got all humane with natural habitats. When you could actually see the animals trapped up close. "Guess they don't want any unauthorized flights," I mumbled as I turned off the ignition and stepped out of my car.

The security guard eyed my outfit as he gave me back my ID and handed me a visitors' badge. Perhaps I shouldn't have worn a low-cut sweater to a military base. I quickly tied my long, brown hair back into a ponytail.

"You need a shot in order to interact with them," he said.

"What? You think I'll get the bird flu from my feathered friend? I'd rather skip it."

"Department of Defense rules, Miss." He stuck me in the arm.

"Mind your manners in there," the guard said gruffly as he put a piece of gauze on my inner elbow. "Don't make any wisecracks. Last guy that went in there made the mistake of calling one of them bird-brained. He didn't look too pretty after that."

I walked into the first hangar and found Robin grinning as a technician ground down his claws using a grinder wheel the size of his head.

"You want a manicure, too?" he said.

"No, thanks. Already got one of the French ones," I said, holding up my white-colored nail tips.

"We gotta grind down our nails before we interact with civilians. Normally, we keep them sharp though, so we are used to it."

"One guy ripped open his face, right after the procedure," the technician said softly. "He had an itch. Almost died."

"Basically, the moral of the story is—don't pick your nose," Robin laughed.

The technician frowned. I couldn't help but stare at the difference between their hands. Almost the same, but Robin's hands had black claws that jutted out several inches from his fingers.

Robin walked me to the bar a few buildings over. He sat on a barstool and tucked his wings in behind him.

"You'd think they wouldn't let us have a bar on base, but they figured out it's easier to keep us here and pretty harmless. We can't even fly after a few gallons," he laughed.

The bartender was drying out the large glasses with a towel. His hand shook as he set down our glasses and slowly poured.

"There you go, Miss," he said, a little too politely. "Rob. No charge."

The other squadron members started to gather around us to say hello. It wasn't the first time men had flocked around me, I thought with a smile, but there was something frightening about all those black wings encircling me.

"We really need more women to join," one of them said. His beady eyes stared at me a little too long.

I stuck out my hand like an idiot and put it back in my pocket. Of course, no one would shake my hand here.

"You wanna go for a ride, honey?"

"Knock it off," Robin said.

Rob and I sat down at the table. I carried his beer for him and put it on the tabletop. It didn't look like it was too easy to carry with those claws in the way. The wooden table had dark patches and rings from all the spills.

"I gotta ask you some hard questions, Rob," I pointed to my list. "I don't want this to turn into a simple propaganda piece. Some of them don't necessarily indicate what I feel, but more along the lines of questions the public has. You understand that, right? I might have to play devil's advocate a bit, but it's nothing personal. You know I believe in what you are doing for this country. Especially with the war."

He nodded and awkwardly sipped his beer. Some foam drizzled down the side as he sat it down on the wooden table.

"First question about signing up… some people want to know. Is this a deal with the devil to live?"

"What was I supposed to do? Just die?" Robin said, just above a whisper.

"That's what most people do," I said. "But I'm glad you're alive."

"Are you?" he said. "My wife says I'm not really human anymore. I'm not who I used to be."

I wrote that down.

"How is she?"

"I don't know. She doesn't want to see me anymore. Says I'm too frightening for the children."

"I'm sorry, Rob."

"But at least I can support them," he said. "Protect them. I still love them, and they know that. At least I'm alive." Robin paused. "It's funny though, the things that used to matter so much, don't matter much anymore. It's different things, more animalistic things…"

"Like what?" I asked.

"Basic things, like eating raw fish from the ocean, sleeping… basic urges."

He leaned forward. "Those guys aren't kidding when they say we need women to join."

I leaned back in my chair and turned red. I picked up my pen again and looked down at the paper.

"What was it like to go from cancer to this?" I asked.

"I don't really want to talk about that," he said. "The cancer. I can tell you what it's like to turn into an animal, though. It doesn't matter what painkillers they give you, when those wings rip out of your shoulder blades, it burns like hell. But it's an amazing feeling when you remember how to fly, like how did I never remember this floating feeling? Why didn't I try before?"

He spread his black wings and stretched out behind him.

"The real philosophical question you have to ask yourself is can you hold on to your humanity when they change your nature? Why care about saving humanity when you're no longer human? Can you remember, or are you just a bird when it all comes down to it? A falcon, a robin, an eagle, a fucking pigeon?"

My pen scratched the paper furiously as I tried to keep up with his words. Vowels and punctuation disappeared. It was a language only I would understand when we were done. After a moment, I looked up from the lined paper and asked my next question.

"When the Christian Peace Activists put up that billboard a mile from the base, calling you guys devils, depicting you as fallen angels, like Lucifer, what was your reaction?"

"Those weren't exactly streaks of white paint on the billboard the next day," Robin grinned. "That's what we thought of it. It hurts. They think we're just a bunch of feathered devils after all we've done for them. But I like the idea of peace, the idea of a world where people like us aren't needed. We're not there, yet."

"What kind of work do you do for the government exactly?"

"You know I can't talk much about that." He leaned back in his stool and pulled his black wings in close to his body.

"After five years of discussing the issue with the United Nations, the US government finally signs the UN accord against using drones, but how are you guys any different from drones when it comes down to it?" My mouth was dry when I said the words taken straight off the pages of my notebook. I was nervous he'd take the question the wrong way.

"We are a lot more accurate when it comes to precision attacks on terrorists," Robin said. "And nothing, I mean nothing, strikes fear into the hearts and minds of terrorists like one of us shooting down to claim him."

"So what's your role in all that, specifically?" I asked. "Have you ever 'claimed' a terrorist?" I wondered if the feathers were soft or razor sharp. It was hard to tell.

"Not yet. I'm actually in charge of recruiting. But to be honest, what we really excel at as a group is surveillance, flying under the radar, so to speak," he said. "The military wants us to fight. But all most of us really want to do is feed. I'm getting hungry right now. Want to fly off with me to get some sushi?"

"Sure." I stared into the bottom of my beer glass.

"Finish it up, Jeannie." He smiled as I chugged the last of the dregs.

The beer tasted strong and bitter. Maybe the alcohol was making me braver. Definitely stupider. I noticed his eyes were still the same old, deep blue.

The maintenance crew outfitted me for the trip with a bulky backpack. "You might get a little wet. The green string is for the life jacket," the crewman said stiffly. "The red one's for the parachute."

I nodded and nervously repeated the words to him.

"It's a fun ride." The crewman mustered a small smile and patted my shoulder. "You'll probably like it."

I tucked my notebook into a sealed plastic bag in my sweater pocket.

Robin stood on the grass runway. "I'm gonna take off and then come back and swoop you up once I've gotten some speed," he said.

Robin started running, then leapt into the air. I expected him to fall flat on his face. But the wings caught the wind, and with slow flaps, he shot higher and higher in the air until he was a speck against the sun.

"Did he forget me?" I laughed.

"Nope," the crewman said. "Now, he's coming for you."

The speck shot straight down. The large, black hulking form came straight at me. I froze like terrified prey. Then he snatched me roughly with his hands and tucked me under his arm. I was too scared to scream.

"Hey, don't forget to breathe, Jeannie. I don't want you passing out on me."

The words made me relax a bit, until I looked down and saw the tiny houses, tiny barracks, toy soldiers, toy tanks, toy planes below.

"You ever want to fly away to a mountain top sometime and hide?" I asked.

"Would you want to come with me, if I did?" he winked. "You know I always had a crush on you in college."

"Did you?"

"But we don't have much in common right now, do we?" he asked. "It's like that old saying from that old movie, 'a bird may love a fish, but where would they live?'"

We soared down into the clouds. I opened my mouth to taste them, but all I felt was moist air, condensation. I half expected to see angels walking along puffy bridges and pathways, the valleys in between white clouds. But there was no one there, just me and Robin.

"I can't breathe very well," I gasped.

"I'll take you down for a bit then," he said.

My feet landed on the rocky ledge. My legs shook, and it took a moment for my muscles to relax. I ran a hand along the tight muscles along my neck and upper back just below the straps of the pack.

"I'm surprised they let me talk to you, Rob. No one ever asks the government questions anymore. Is it strange that they let me see you?"

"I'll be honest with you. It wasn't an accident you saw that picture." He started to preen his feathers with his teeth, then stopped. "I don't know if they'll let you leave or not. Maybe if you write what they want you to write. Or maybe they just want you to join."

"Is that a threat?" My shout echoed against the rocks.

"You don't seem very thrilled by that idea."

I took a step back against the rocky wall of the cliff. There wasn't much room to maneuver on the ledge. I gripped the straps of my pack.

"In fact, they are tracking you right now," he said. "Give me that." He grabbed the pack off my back, ripping the straps. His claws were growing sharper by the minute.

I watched as the camouflage pack fell down hundreds of feet and crashed into the foamy waves. It floated for a moment and then disappeared under the froth and rocks.

"My stuff!" I yelled. "Fuck."

"You've got other things to worry about, besides losing your wallet and phone," Robin said. "I've got other things to worry about. Christ, I'm so hungry. I can't take it anymore." He grabbed me under one arm and dove into the water.

It felt like my stomach lurched into my chest. My heart pounded. There was wind, specks of dirt or bugs flying into my eyes, salty humid air, then foamy seawater, bubbles, and claws reaching for life in the dark depths.

The whole while, I held my breath and felt my chest constricted under his arm, gripped under that elbow. There was nothing bird-like about him. It was like being crushed by a monster.

When we emerged from the water, he dragged me to a cave just above the waves.

He gripped a squid the size of a basketball in his claws and hungrily dug his face in. His teeth punctured the rubbery arms with a popping sound. Juices squirted out. He grinned as he swallowed white chunks of flesh.

"Sorry," he said. "Where are my manners? Did you want some? It's delicious."

My stomach turned rancid as I watched him eat the rest of his meal. White gelatin-like flesh was caught in the right corner of his mouth.

He noticed me looking. "What, you want a kiss?" He laughed and wiped his mouth with his arm.

"I should take you back to the base now," he said.

"I'm afraid," I said, looking down at the water lapping the rocks.

"You can't stay here," he said. "Tide's coming in."

He took me under his arm and slowly flew off over a sandy beach. I looked down and saw the white caps lapping the shore. Gray water. It felt peaceful.

"Can you drop me off downtown?" I added an address I knew.

"What do I look like? A taxi driver?" Robin said. "I'll leave you at the edge of the city, close to a road. I wouldn't go back to the base for your truck. I'd try to keep a low profile if I were you for a while. Try to disappear."

I said nothing, but I thought that was the worst idea of all, knowing this administration. The address I had given him was for a broadcast TV station. I knew someone in the news department there. Maybe they'd want an interview. Maybe if I were in the public eye, I could avoid being snatched by the government. It might provide some kind of protection rather than disappearing quietly.

He lowered me by a road. I was so happy to see the black asphalt. I could breathe again as I walked along that road, felt the ground under my feet. I rubbed my aching back muscles. I pulled off the gauze on my inner elbow and noticed the puffy, itchy red mark from the shot. It had been a rough ride.

"Best of luck," Robin said. "If you somehow see them, tell my children I'm not the monster they think I am, and I'm not the monster the government wants me to be."

"Thanks for helping me escape."

"I'm sorry I couldn't do more," he said and ran.

"Aren't you worried about me getting to where I'm going?" I asked as he leapt into the air and flew off. Maybe he didn't hear me.

I walked down the road until it started to get dark. I could hear crickets, frogs croaking, and an owl hooting in trees. My back ached so bad, I bent over and rubbed it with one hand. I flagged down an old truck driving my way.

The driver, a heavy-set man with bushy brown eyebrows and sun-spotted arms, swung open the passenger door.

"Your car break down?" he asked.

I shook my head.

"You've got no business walking in the dark with all the animals in the area, young lady," he said.

I climbed into the front seat and sighed in relief. It felt good to be in a safe, warm place. As I undid my salty, wet ponytail, I pulled a small, black feather out of my hair. It was soft. Then I found another black feather.

"Man," I said. "I'm so hungry."

I looked down at my dirty hands and noticed my French manicure was gone. I tried to wipe the black dirt off my nails, but it was hopeless.

"I'm so hungry," I said.

"You want a granola bar?" The man opened his glove compartment.

"No, thanks." I wrinkled my nose in disgust at the idea.

I kept rubbing my neck and my aching upper back with my hands. The muscles were tightening up and spasming, then burning. I gasped in and felt my whole body constrict as bones and flesh and bloody feathers sliced through my back. The car window shattered as my wings unfolded.

"Holy fucking shit," the driver said, trying to push my left wing out of his face with his arm. He lost control of the truck and veered into the ditch, into waist-high weeds.

I got out. My sweater had shredded into black rags when the wings sliced through. I took the largest piece and tied it around my breasts.

It didn't hurt as much as Robin had said. Maybe it's true that women have a higher pain tolerance than men. But I fumed with anger, seethed so much my jawbones clenched together. They had changed me against my will. I didn't say anything to the man in the truck. Neither of us seemed to have any words left. He just stared with his mouth open so wide you could see almost all of his crooked, lower teeth.

I started to run and then remembered how to fly. The black wings unfolded with a whoosh, like of a giant sail opening, and I leapt into the air, flapping higher and higher, circling until the truck and the man were tiny insignificant specs on the ground. He became a mere scurrying insect.

I circled back to the cliff and leapt headfirst. The winds screamed into my ears, and then I felt the pressure change with a pop as I shot down into the icy sea. When I emerged with a pale, white squid, I tore through it in chunks. The legs popped and leaked delicious salty juices into my mouth. Rubbery, slimy deliciousness oozed down the back of my throat. I was no longer angry, no longer afraid, just hungry and happy to feed. That was all that mattered to me now. I didn't remember anything else. I didn't care about anything else. The war had disappeared. Civilization had disappeared. I was just a bird flying away.

Lost in The Poet's Garden

I AM CRYING SOFTLY, lost in the lushness of a Van Gogh, The Poet's Garden to be exact. Branches, swathed in green droop in the corner. Leaves swirl in hues of mustard yellow and musty green. A few pink blossoms pop in the distance. There is beauty here, strangling under a sickly green sky and discord drizzling down from a distant sun. I walk through wet stalks of grass. I grasp prickly madness in these bushes. The whole world is framed in despondent green, peppered with crazy orange. You can see God's brushstrokes if you get close enough. You can become a stroke.

I want to escape these swirls, to break this canvas. There must be other colors outside of this pallet, outside of this world. I see a tiny silvery blue piece in the distance, an unreachable peak like a faraway mountain.

How could he know how I felt in that moment? How do you escape a moment, when it's a masterpiece made by a tortured genius who has seen and predicted your very soul?

When I close my eyes, I see this picture. For years, I have seen it. I close my eyes—it lingers. I open them and pull out a knife.

The security guard in the corner, a woman in an ill-fitting black suit, white shirt, and a tie, pops into my frame of vision screaming. "Stop! Put the knife down." The sound echoes off the museum walls.

"I don't want to ever feel this way again," I say. "Don't you understand? This is a picture of pain, and it's taken me over. I don't want to ever feel green again."

She spreads her arms out across in front of me, like she'd take a knife plunging into her heart for the sake of art.

"Stop," she says.

I step forward, push her out of my way, and slash, one more stroke, against a canvas laden with them. The canvas splits, a gaping mouth devouring me into the dark shadows behind it. Is she screaming or me? Or is it the painting? Where is the sound coming from?

A man comes up behind me and grips me from the back. I drop the knife, sobbing. Because even though he has pulled me away, I'm destined to walk here forever. There's no escaping this greenery. My prison, my fate, has opened and swallowed me whole.

Arsonist Housewife

I SING A GARBLED VERSION of Billy Joel's "We Didn't Start the Fire" and poke holes in the plastic film on a frozen entrée with a fork. I load the black tray into the microwave and start attacking dishes in the sink. A pan stares back at me with crusts of black gunk caked across its Teflon like the angry surface of a torched planet. I quickly toss it aside. After all, I only have three to five minutes to tackle the sink.

But then again, I will need to wash all the dishes before my husband gets home. Or he won't have sex with me. Not that doing the dishes is a guarantee of sex, mind you. Just that not doing the dishes is a recipe for a dry spell, for sure, and I kind of want to stay married. I do love him. In marriage counseling, he had asked for a clean house. Which might sound sexist, except for the fact that he hadn't been home for three days on a business trip in this case, and the mess is usually mine. I had reveled in breaking the rules, in leaving the sink full while he was gone. But now it's time to make up for it.

So I start attacking the Teflon. Fun fact: The chemicals used in making Teflon are in all of our bodies now. But this pan predates that knowledge. Its handle is charred, as well, and loose. It's decades old, an artifact, really. I should just throw this away. But instead I embark on a salvage operation. The blue sponge turns black in my hands. Flakes of black wash away, revealing more black below. I continue singing, mumbling new words to the old song I have half forgotten.

"We were always flirting since the town's been burning," I sing off-key. "Something something Nixon. Something, something, something pigeons."

The surface of the pan emerges below my soapy fingers. "There, good as new," I say, with a triumphant smile, hanging it up on the rack. For a moment, I think of my marriage. Like a clean pan is some kind of metaphor for our relationship. There's nothing sexy about a clean pan, I think sadly.

I wonder if our marriage counselor would disagree? She wore stilettos to our appointments and short skirts, showcasing her long, lean legs. She wore an engagement ring for a while, and then the ring disappeared from her hand. For all I know she has never been married for a day in her life. What does she know about raising twin boys and trying to keep the spark alive? The boys are at preschool in the afternoons, in the hopes of teaching the wild beasts social skills. It is a miracle the entire house isn't more trashed than it is.

I can hear the marriage counselor in my head. "Maybe if you focus on his needs, by keeping a cleaner house, he will be more attentive to your emotional needs," she said.

"I'm absent minded. I don't even notice these things. Why can't he just accept me the way I am?" I recall my own words back. And then there was the impossibility of keeping a house clean with two small, identical tornadoes. I should've punched her in her perfect makeup-covered face.

This is the part where I notice the smell, realize I set the microwave at thirty minutes instead of three, just an extra zero and a preoccupied mind. I open its door, and black smoke billows out. I reach for the frozen entrée and immediately drop it. It splatters and gurgles onto the floor. The plastic wrap has disintegrated. I let out a few curse words, run cold water on my hands. Then I notice, the microwave oven itself has a flickering flame within it, smoldering and smoking. I debate dumping water on it. Is it an electrical fire? Should I get a fire extinguisher? Oh crap, where do I keep that sucker, anyway? I search under the sink and find it wedged in the back.

My eyes sting from the smoke as I try to read the instructions on the fire extinguisher. I pull the plastic ring and it twists off in my hands. Umm, was that supposed to happen? I shriek. I push the handle and nothing happens.

The flame is spreading to the wall. If I die, will my husband take back all those things he's said about me being dirty? If I hadn't tried to clean the pan, none of this would have happened.

"We Didn't Start the Fire" continues playing in my head. I'd sing along but it's not quite true. I didn't set the fire, but I am responsible in my negligence. Oh screw the electrical fire, I say and pull out the spray nozzle from the sink. The plastic tubing extends as far as it can but it's not far enough. I spray and the water stops short by about a foot. Maybe I'm meant to die here. I cough. I grab a pitcher from the cupboard and fill it with water, I splash the microwave and wall. I can feel the steam against my face as it hits the fire and sizzles. I repeat. I think I've got most of it, but I can still hear crackling in the wall. I call 911.

"What's the emergency?" The dispatcher asks.

"My kitchen wall caught on fire. I think I've got most of it out, but I'm not sure."

I hear keys and the clicking of opening locks. My husband is home.

"Hey, what's going on?" he coughs. "Did you, did you start a fire?"

"If you hadn't asked for a clean house, none of this would have happened," I say. I have reached a new stage of not giving a flying fig. I grab a bottle of wine, and a wine opener out of the drawer.

"It's smoky and hazy in here—let's go outside and sit on the curb while we wait for the firetruck," I say.

Sirens wail in the distance. "Look, this clean house thing," I start, opening the bottle. "It's just not realistic. Why don't we hire some cleaning ladies? They're cheaper than marriage counseling and less dangerous than me cleaning the house." I take a swig from the wine bottle.

"Okay," he says. "I'm just glad you're okay."

"So you aren't angry," I say.

He shakes his head.

"I've wanted to remodel the kitchen for a long time anyway," he says. For a change, he puts his arms around me tight, and for a split second, I close my eyes and think, everything's going to be okay. And maybe, just maybe, if it means he'll hold me like this, I should set the house on fire more often.

A One-Star Review

THE SERVICE LAST NIGHT at Ollie's Lobster and Fish was simply unacceptable.

Much to my chagrin, my wife and I were seated next to the kitchen door. As the door swung open and closed with the servers whisking food in and out, midway through the meal, we caught sight of something truly disturbing in the kitchen. Not a rat, not a mouse, it was a squirrel. A squirrel with beady little eyes. One of the cooks in the kitchen was feeding it. Had even named it Bill. She was saying, "sweet, Bill, what a cutie you are." That was when Bill looked up and stared at me, stared into my very soul. It was like a challenge.

I asked my server. "Isn't it a health code violation to have a squirrel in the kitchen?"

She shrugged. "I'll let the manager know."

Bill cocked his head and stared at me harder still, before the door swung closed again. When it reopened, Bill was no longer perched on the stainless-steel counter. He was on the ground. Bill boldly approached me, thwacking his tail against the wooden floorboards. "I wonder what he's saying in squirrel language?" I said to my wife, laughing.

"Maybe he understood your threat to call a city inspector," she said.

I turned to my wife, and said, "What's a squirrel gonna do about it?"

That was when Bill leapt for my face. I could feel tiny squirrel hands on my mouth. I struck him, and he flew through the air, landing in my butternut squash and shrimp soup. Now, Bill was covered in orange.

"What's wrong with you?" I asked Bill. It was more rhetorical than anything.

"Honey, he's a squirrel," my wife said.

"What kind of a place is this?" I bellowed.

I asked the server to bring me more soup sans squirrel. Her hands were shaking as she took the old bowl away. In fear of Bill or of me? I realized she was afraid of me! I was made to feel like I was some kind of monster when all I wanted was a bowl of butternut squash and shrimp soup.

To my surprise, the server patted Bill with a white cloth napkin, picked Bill up, and put him in her shirt pocket. The kitchen door swung open and closed. When the soup came out, it was delicious, except when I got to the bottom. What did I find? Squirrel droppings.

Eating the Storm

STANDING AT THE EDGE OF THE FIELD, staring into the horizon, Sara swallowed the approaching storm. She unhinged her jaw and swallowed wide, dislocating it. A shooting pain crept up her face. The gray storm clouds tasted salty in her mouth. The condensation slid down the back of her throat, a downpour that threatened to drown her. Her belly swelled, swirled, distended with a hard rain.

A control freak, always trying to please other people. Now she was trying to control the weather. What would her therapist think?

Sara furrowed her brow, clamped her teeth together despite the shooting pain. She was afraid that it would escape. That it would hurt all the people she loved, so she held it in.

The hair on the back of her neck rose, the hair on her arms too. Tiny, fine, blond hairs. She stared at them with wild wide eyes. Afraid if she spoke, the opening of her mouth would release it. She whimpered slightly, but no one was there to hear her.

Sara pushed back the urge to vomit and felt the storm churn within her. Her shoulder-length hair now stood on end. She reached up and tried to pull it back down, to no avail.

Her arms and legs swelled. Her feet and hands bloated. Blood vessels blossomed red across expanding skin. The dress she was wearing stretched and constricted her growing frame. The threads broke, shredding across her chest.

Watching her arms and legs balloon, she was afraid she would pop.

She remembered what her therapist had said, "Depression is anger turned inwards."

You'd think these words could have helped her stop it, to let it go, but they didn't.

The thunder rumbled through her internal organs, shaking her liver like jelly, while the lightning sizzled her brain. When they found Sara later, she was never quite the same. Her jaw made strange clicking noises, for one.

Thunder Cloud

HER BACK WAS TO THE DOOR, but she still knew it was him when he walked into the coffee shop. She felt the icy draft from the snowstorm blow in. Heard the noise as the door shut behind him, the shuffle of heavy boots. She looked down at her cup of tea, cradling the warm ceramic, pretending to be lost in her own world. When she looked up, there he was, standing next to the table.

The snow had caught in his dark hair, flecks disappearing white. She wanted to call him names, ask him why he made her feel the way she did, as though he had the answers. Instead, she asked him how he was. And he told her he was good, and she wondered if it was true.

"Please tell me you drove."

"I borrowed a car from a friend."

"Good," she said. "I wouldn't want you to catch pneumonia."

We can never be friends, she wanted to say. But instead complained about the weather. The cold. The snow. The crush of it coming down.

Like the sky had burst. Black windows, condensation, streaks of white. He glanced sideways away from her from time to time.

Look me in the eye, she wanted to say. *Look me in the eye and tell me you never loved me.*

Instead they talked about their jobs and common friends. He still wore the same leather jacket. His hair wasn't as wild. There were things they never talked about, things that never seemed to come up. Her husband. His girlfriend.

"How's your son?" he asked.

"Great."

"How old is he now?"

"Three," she said. "He talks a lot these days. Yesterday, he said 'tomorrow I'll be a thundercloud,' and I thought that was so beautiful and poetic. Tomorrow, I'll be a thundercloud."

As time went on, they took off their coats, unwrapping the layers. She kept smiling, doing that thing where she subliminally traced the edge of her cup with her fingertip in a slightly suggestive fashion. She caught herself doing it, stopped, then started again. He leaned back in his wooden chair, tilted it slightly off the ground, and put his hands behind his head. Did he know he was showing off his arms?

The hours whirled around them. You could measure them in inches outside on the ground.

Finally, she looked at her phone and noticed she had been gone too long.

They wandered out in the cold and out of earshot of the baristas.

"It's no good."

"What's that?"

"We can't be friends," she said.

"You're still interested in me?"

"Interested. Interested, is that how you put it?" Her face flushed.

"We can never be friends," she repeated.

"We can never be anything else."

"You misunderstand me," she said. "I'm not looking for anything."

"Then why did you want to meet up?" he said.

"We had unfinished business."

"Is it finished now?" He unlocked the car and opened the door.

"Yes," she said.

If he had offered her a ride, would she have taken it?

No, he wasn't her friend.

Paper Dolls

HE WASN'T THE PRETTIEST BOY. It was an unfortunate fact of life. He remembered the age when he stopped being cute, around three or four. The cooing and smiles from strangers stopped. As a teenager, his neck grew long like a giraffe, dotted by a heavy Adam's apple—its dancing mesmerized him in the mirror. It was like a trapped creature about to burst out of a horror film. He wore thick glasses that magnified his brown eyes to epic sci-fi proportions. The hairs of his brows knitted together at the center.

And yet, he was in love with the prettiest girl in chemistry class. She was his opposite. Other than her long blond hair, her body was completely hairless while his was hirsute. She was tan. He was pale.

She just happened to sit by him when it came time for the labs. He must have looked smart. The irony was that he wasn't particularly intelligent in her presence. The words came out in an awkward garble. He was too distracted to focus on the professor. In fact, he found himself copying her work, drumming his fingers on the black tabletop, and daydreaming.

One day, after class she forgot her notebook. It had slid out of the bottom of her bag and was just sitting there on the ground. He picked it up, flipped open the red cover. The first page had private written in bold black marker, and he quickly flipped past.

The strange thing was that there were drawings of men in there, handsome men, naked men, ripped men, more average. Some looked tall. Some looked short. Then there he was. She had edited nothing. His nose was ginormous. But his long hair flowed in waves. The curve of his gut. The skinniness of his arms. It was all there, but the inclusion was puzzling. He was no object of beauty. He did not belong among the flowers and doodles of stars. He did not belong in those lined pages.

She had sketches of clothes on some pages. Was she a fashion design major of some kind?

He emailed her. Hey, you forgot something in class, a notebook. Do you want me to drop it off at your dorm?

Her reply was one word: Yes. Followed by the dormitory name and room number.

He'd never been in a girl's dormitory before, never been invited, and he wasn't about to show up without an invitation.

It was strange she hadn't thanked him. Maybe she was embarrassed. When he opened the door, would she be naked? The thought flitted into his head. He imagined her doing so. It was a harmless little daydream.

But when she opened the door, she was fully clothed, a bit breathless. She pushed a lock of blond hair back behind her ear. She wore a purple sweater that swallowed her curves, over a pair of skinny jeans that outlined her sleek calf muscles.

"Ray," she said, opening the door.

He held the notebook in his hand, but he didn't dare hand it over, not yet. He was going to prolong the exchange as long as possible. As long as he could. It might be the only time he had a chance to really talk to her.

"Jessica," he said. "How are you?"

That's what he meant to say. But instead, the words came out differently.

"Jessica," he said. "Why did you draw me?"

"Wow, you can't read, can you? I wrote private on that. You wanna read my journal too now? Looking at my drawings is pretty much the same thing."

"I'm sorry. I was curious. But why did you draw me?"

"I'm an artist," she said. "That's what we do. We draw things."

"Am I a thing?" he asked.

She smirked. "Have a seat, if you like," she said. "Do you want a beer?"

He couldn't believe she was sitting down next to him on the bed, the tiny dormitory bed.

"What do you want?" she said. "Help with your homework? I've noticed you struggling."

"I don't know that I'm satisfied with your answer," he said. "Why did you draw me?"

"Look, you've got a distinctive look," she said. "I draw a lot of guys."

"What do you do with them?" he said.

"The drawings or the guys?"

"The drawings," he said, but also the men, he wondered, what did she do to them? With them?

"Let me show you," she said.

She took a pair of scissors and cut out his figure, then cut out the drawings of clothes. To his surprise, they overlapped.

"You turned me into a paper doll?"

"Yes," she said with a shrug.

She kept cutting the other men out, cutting out their clothes.

"Why do you like to draw men?" he asked.

"Because I like to imagine what they could look like, under different circumstances. What they'd look like with different clothes, without their clothes."

As he gulped, he could feel his Adam's apple leap up along his neck.

"You are a strange girl," he said.

"I'm a strange woman," she said.

"What about me? Would you like to see me in different clothes? Without my clothes, in real life? You can draw me anyway you like."

She laughed. "Seriously?"

"Seriously," he said.

"You want to be treated like a plaything?"

"I don't mind," he said. It was the truth. He didn't mind at all.

"Fine, then take off your clothes," she said.

He removed his T-shirt, revealing his pale chest. There was more hair surrounding the left nipple than the right. He removed his belt and flung it onto the floor with a kind of violence.

"Aren't you afraid?" he asked.

"No," she said. "I'm not afraid. The walls are so thin a million people would hear me scream if I did. Are you afraid?"

He nodded, then unzipped his pants.

Now, God had given him some gifts, but he covered himself with his hands. "Do I look like you imagined?"

"A little." She took out her sketchpad.

"What if your roommate comes back?" he asked.

"She's seen me sketch before," she said.

He bent his head down awkwardly. His shoulders hunched forward. He covered himself. He felt humiliated, but also a strange flame burned inside him. Even if she was just playing with him, it felt good to be played with, good to have someone paying attention to him for a change. It was a strange little game they were playing. He wondered where it would lead.

"Stand up straight," she commanded. "Shoulders back."

He shifted his spine into position, but not enough. It surprised him when she put her hands on him, moved his shoulders back, put her hand in the small of his back, and gave it a gentle push.

"Why are you doing this?" he said. "I'm not pretty."

"Pretty boys are overrated," she said. "Besides, doesn't everyone deserve a little love?"

"Is that what this is," he asked. "A form of love?"

"I don't know," she said. "Maybe a form of admiration."

"What do you admire about me?"

"The way you don't give a crap when the professor's talking," she said. "Like you are in a different world half the time."

"I'm in your world," he said, softly. It felt strange to admit, but something about taking off his clothes had made him bold. He was already naked. It didn't matter what he admitted.

"Love is like a set of clothes," she murmured. "You put it on a person, and it completely changes the way they look. You take it away, and they look completely different."

He laughed.

"Did that sound pretentious?" she asked. "I'm not trying to sound deep. I'm just thinking out loud. I do that when I work."

"Can I see? You know, you look like you come out of a catalog, like you belong in a catalog."

"You want to mail order me?" she asked. "Why do men and

women treat each other like pieces of meat to be consumed?"

"Because consuming each other is a lot of fun," he said.

"You think I'm pretty. What if I weren't? What if one of these days, I get maimed in a horrible car accident, or get old? Then I'll seem fundamentally different. You, on the other hand."

"What, I already look maimed?" he asked.

"That's unkind," she said. "That's not what I meant."

"But it's the truth, an inconvenient fact," he said.

"A pretty girl and an ugly boy don't mix," he said. "There's no love story to be written about that, not unless I'm a millionaire."

"What about *Beauty and the Beast*?" she asked. "I always liked that Disney film the best. There's something rugged about you."

"Ragged, more likely," he said. He couldn't shake the feeling she was teasing him. "Besides, the beast had a castle."

"Material wealth and looks aren't everything," she said.

"Aren't they?" he joked, wandering closer to her. He reached for her pencil and set it down on her desk. He reached for her arm and pulled her to him.

He tried to kiss her, but she pulled away.

She reached for the scissors on the table.

"Are you going to cut me?" he asked, backing off. "That's hardly necessary."

"No," she said. "Of course not. It's just you're so …"

"Ugly," he said.

"No, naked," she said. "This seems to be moving swiftly, don't you think? I mean, I've had people get the wrong idea before when doing these sketches."

"So, I really am a plaything, then?" he asked. "A paper doll, an amusement?"

She bit her lip.

"Put your clothes back on, please," she said.

He obliged. Put on his pants, stumbling as he did so. Pulled on his T-shirt. He wished he looked differently.

He turned to walk out the door, and she stopped him.

"What would you look like if I covered you with love?" she said, and caressed the side of his face. "I don't know." She sighed.

"You're too shallow to try," he said bitterly.

"Who is the shallow one?" she asked. "You don't know me. You just like me for my looks. What's more shallow? Loving someone for beauty or not loving them for ugliness?"

"We are both paper dolls, aren't we?" he said with a smirk. "I get what you're trying to say."

"Don't leave yet," she said. "Dance with me."

She turned on the music, and it was Radiohead's "Creep."

It was an odd choice. The song was slow and melodic, and as the singer, Thom Yorke, rang out with a moan, and he found himself singing along about being a creep and not being able to look her in the eye.

"Your voice makes you beautiful," she said. "You have a beautiful voice."

Then she laid her head on his shoulder, and the two paper dolls danced together into the night, like two pieces of paper caught in the same sudden gust of wind. The music had a way of twirling them around.

How Tim Wilson Lost His Corner Office

INITIALLY, TIM WASN'T UPSET when the long, slithering black limb smashed through his corner office window. It was Friday after a long week, and he wanted to go home early, anyway. The gravity of the situation didn't hit him until the limb shot through the room and tore Judy, his assistant, out the window, flinging her to the ground, three stories down. He ducked under his desk, gasping for breath. He gripped his favorite pen in his hand and prepared to stab the monster if it reached for him next. Not that a pen would do much good against it.

He knew he should stay where he was, but he couldn't help but peek out from under the mahogany wood. Tim saw a giant eye looking at him. Just one. Gray as smoke. He could feel its icy breath against his face. He knew he needed time to run, but before he could think, he lashed out with the pen, stabbing the creature in the eye. Tim heard what sounded like a roar or squeal really as he flung open his office door.

"That was for Judy!" he said. God, he hoped she landed on something soft. Injuries would make it hard for them to continue their affair. Inside the stairwell, he spiraled farther and farther down. He could hear the monster thrashing, the sound of broken glass, and splintering wood.

Concrete started crumbling behind him. The entire building shook violently with each blow. Tim darted out into the parking lot, and found his car, with the top torn off. I always wanted a convertible, he thought. God, I hope Judy is okay. Unfortunately, she wasn't. She was fatality No. 1.

He drove off, going 130 mph on city streets. Every bump caused him to flinch. The air whooshed inside the vehicle. When he got back to his house, he inspected the damage to his beloved BMW. Where did this cantaloupe come from? He wondered, looking at the melon in the back seat.

He touched it and felt the small indentations dotting across its grayish-brown surface.

Wait, a second, it's not a cantaloupe, he realized. It was warm to the touch. It was splitting and hatching in his hands. Looking in, he saw a small gray eye, peering at him. He wondered if the newborn creature was innocent. Briefly, it reminded him of when his son was born. That was before it expelled poison all over his face from its butthole.

The Hoarder

THE ROOM IS DARK EXCEPT for the flying toasters. They glow in the dark, darting back and forth with their angel wings across the oversized computer screen, circa 1987. Except it isn't 1987.

I get up and tap at the keys.

"Sleep, go to sleep," I whisper. But the blue streaks, the black in flickering vertical lines, and a layer of dust flies up from the giant computer's chest. It won't turn off.

I want to hit the machine, but I know it will break. "I don't want you to sleep forever, just for the night," I whisper like it's a baby in need of love and attention. It's three a.m., and the toasters will not relinquish control of the room, a nightlight gone mad driving me mad.

The station that the oversized monitor is stacked upon, like a heap of plastic sculpture, crooked and heavy and awkward, was never beautiful—not even brand-new state-of-the-art never art, but still a monstrous beauty in the form of bulk aesthetic horror.

And so the fluttering, flying toasters return, lighting up the room, flickering across my closed eyelids. And I wonder, why have I taken this relic into my home? Have I caught the hoarder's disease, the inability to let go of the past?

I found the beast in a heap of garbage at the back of the hoarder's house yesterday. I walked with it, juggled it, took it home, and I plugged it in, the thick cord coiled over my shoulder. It took me two trips. The base of it weighed a good forty pounds and made my arms sag.

It has this gray-beige color that makes it look dirty no matter what you do. I don't know if they were always this color or if time made them that way—the lines on the sides, the lines on the bottom. You wonder about why, the vents, breathing loud whooshing breaths, the holes, the pins, the slots for discs you can't find anymore. Where do you find those things? What are they called? Floppies? Black, plastic rectangles with silver metal parts.

Maybe I should go back, I think. Maybe I should go back and see what else she's got out there. Because really, it's sitting under a blue tarp in the rain and it isn't really stealing because she shouldn't have it there. She has too much stuff, and it's killing her, and one day it's all going to crush her and those cats. The cats you see slinking around with their tails and backs and fur hiked up. I want to go back to the house with the white, peeling paint.

I wonder if it's my conscience keeping me up. No. Just the flying toasters. Maybe there's a printer out there somewhere, I think, and slip into sleep. Maybe some floppies. I could use them as decorative coasters, repurpose them, create something new from the hulks of plastic.

The next day I get up and walk by the old lady's house. I don't care about going to school anymore, just what I can find. I toss on my backpack over one shoulder and get ready to rummage. There I am in her backyard, rifling through the black trash bags, standing on the dead, brown grass.

It's like a field of crap or a museum of memories. I can't make up my mind how to phrase it. There are bags of old, yellow, moldy newspapers. Bags of plastic bags. Collections of stuffed animals missing eyes, with fluffy tails gone scraggly. Torn, black plastic covers the windows, hiding what's inside the house. In the yard, an army of folding chairs is lined up in rows waiting for a concert that will never grace the roof of the garage. I open a trash bag full of plastic cases, and there they are.

I got it, I think with a laugh. I got the discs. For some reason, this makes me happy. Like I've found a piece of history, reclaimed a piece of obscurity, like an archaeologist finding dinosaur bones. I find the printer under the tarp and sling it under one arm. It's still got a ream of paper, the kind with the edges you tear off and the little holes. It's all yellow, but it's there still like a prime museum piece.

"Hey, sonny boy," the woman's voice calls from the back porch. "You want to see my gun collection, too?"

She's about sixty, and she's got a handgun in each hand, and her mouth is forming a hard, straight line across her face. Her hair is parted down the middle and hangs long and gray in waves.

"Give me back my discs," she says.

I don't think, just bolt, and I don't care that my sneaker laces are undone, and I don't care that she's scrambling out of her house, and I can hear her shoes across the wooden boards of her porch.

I'm running and running, and I don't care about the printer, but it's still pinned under my arm. Inside my head, I'm wondering, Jesus Christ lady, what could possibly be on those discs, possibly be on this computer? Was she some sort of hippie psychopath who took pictures of her victims and never deleted the evidence?

What is on the computer that's so important? Why would anyone care so much about a piece of junk sitting out back in their yard under a tarp, enough to pull two guns?

I'm sweating, and I can hear a truck engine behind me, and I know it's her, and I'm running, and she's driving next to me, and I'm on the sidewalk, and she's got this smirk on her worn leather face.

"Come on, kid, give it up," she says. "I'm not going to shoot you, I don't think."

I stop running, and her truck comes to a squeaky stop.

"Get in the truck, kid," she says. "I'll give you a ride."

I stare at her dubiously for a minute, but she does remind me of my grandma.

"Listen, I'm going to drive you to your house, and you are gonna give me back my computer, kid. Then we're even. I won't try to kill you."

I raise my chin. I'm not a kid.

"Sounds fair, I guess," I say, and I do something stupid—I get in the rusty old Ford.

"I'm sorry," I say breathlessly in the passenger side. "I didn't think you needed it."

I'm in the old lady's truck, and there are thousands of receipts on the passenger side. Crumpled, twisted pieces of paper everywhere in a rustling pile of yellow, white, and faded ink letters and numbers. It's like the paper version of a ball playroom at a cheesy fast food kids' play area. I can feel the receipts behind my knees. I'm surprised there aren't other kinds of trash floating around in the car. Old, half-eaten chicken wings.

"I like to hold on to things," she explains. "Hold on to where I've been, what I've done. That's how you remember."

"But at some point, don't you have to let things go?" I ask.

"You'll understand when you're older," she snarls.

And we drive to my house, and I fumble with my keys, and we climb the white, carpeted steps to my room, and there it is, the beast, with its flying toasters, sitting on my desk in my room.

And the woman with her gray hair sinks to her most likely arthritic knees.

"Oh my god," she says. "It still works. I could never get the damn thing to turn on. I thought it was dead."

And so she straightens up and then sits down in my leather chair, swivels back and forth like a schoolgirl, taps on the keyboard, and the flying toasters vanish and the folders open, and she's reading document after document with tears running down her face.

"It's my old writing, my old poetry," she says. "I thought I lost it."

She's in my room all day clicking through files. The machine is breathing loudly. She is breathing loudly. It is strange. I can still see the butt of a handgun jutting out of one of her pockets.

I wonder what my parents would think of it if they came home to see me with a heavily armed senior citizen in my room. I imagine my mother teasing me about bringing a "girl" home, not noticing the gun. She is a tad inobservant, sometimes, my mother. She never asked where my old gadgets came from.

And then the old lady turns on the printer, and it buzzes to shriek and sing. A dizzy, repetitious noise, and I am so happy as the words spill out that I didn't come from that time because Jesus Christ it was loud and there were flying toasters and bad poems and the museum piece is very much alive and well with her two handguns.

When it comes time to say goodbye, I go to pull the cord, and she grabs my arm and stops me.

"I don't think it's going to turn on again next time," she says. "It was a fluke. Keep it."

I thank her and walk her out. Watch her Ford truck drive off. Sigh, happy not to be shot and murdered. And I climb back up into my room, and there they are, the flying toasters, flying till all of eternity. And I'm a little afraid to pull the plug now—a little afraid the old lady will come back and shoot me if I do because she doesn't believe in letting go of the past.

The only thing the beast is good for is word processing, you know, but not even that, because it's a dead-end. There's only so much paper left. So this hulk of plastic and glass, what it really is now, is a nightlight, a source of light to keep you from tripping in the dark. I don't know when it's going to die out, but I know I'm not going to mess with the museum of memories anymore.

Friends Having Coffee

TWO FRIENDS MEET IN A COFFEE SHOP two days after they each died.

"What a strange coincidence," the first one says.

"That we should die on the same day."

The second one laughs. "I couldn't let you have all the attention."

The first one went by bus, hit by the CTA.

The other one had a weak heart.

Both routes led to the same destination.

"What did you see when you died?" the second one asks.

"A bright, blinding light," the other one says. "What did you see?"

"I saw you reaching out your hand," the second one says.

"Curious," the first one says.

"Is it?" the second one says.

"I don't remember that."

"Where did you go? Heaven or hell?"

"The funny thing is you get to choose. I did not expect that. I went to neither destination," she says.

"I chose to live again," says the second. "I came back as a mourning dove. It didn't last long."

"Why is that?"

"There are owls."

Famished

I WAS THIRTEEN when the hunger pangs began. I wanted so badly to be normal. And yet the cravings for human flesh made that impossible. I bet you think I'm a vampire or a werewolf or something stupid like that. I'm not. I am a monster without a name. Mom said it happens to all girls of our kind, but I think she was just trying to make me feel better.

There was this boy at school, Anthony. He was older than me. He kept coming up behind me and snapping my bra straps. I still remember the fabric pulling my breast roughly upward and the hard sting across my shoulder. Once the clasp in the front of my bra actually came undone and I rushed to the bathroom, crying, feeling exposed with my breasts hanging, nipples unleashed, pointed beneath my shirt. Some of the boys in the class laughed. The girls crossed their arms, but didn't say anything. They were afraid they'd be next.

I complained to the teacher, Mr. Wilson. "Boys will be boys," he said to me quietly with a sigh. "Detention," he said to him loudly. Anthony called me a bitch under his breath for ratting on him.

I waited for him to get out of detention outside the double-doors and led him beneath the bleachers in the field outside after school. "I want to talk to you," I said. "Alone." I remember looking at his face. Anthony had dark hair and cloudy blue eyes mirroring the sky. "What are you looking at?" he asked.

I didn't say anything. My stomach was in knots.

"What do you want to talk about?" he asked. "I'm not saying sorry… I'm not sorry. Are you playing with me?"

"I don't know," I said. "Mom always said not to play with my food." I smiled.

Anthony looked confused. You could see the faint beginnings of facial hair lining his jaw and upper lip. He was a head taller than me and would have been cute if he hadn't been such an asshole. You wouldn't think he would smell so appetizing, a meaty, sweaty smell. I must've made him nervous. I think he thought I was going in for a kiss. I leaned in and inhaled his aroma.

I felt conflicted. A part of me wanted him to like me. Another part was furious and wanted him to treat me with respect. And then there was the hunger. I felt weak and unsteady, had for weeks.

I opened my mouth wide, my whole face really, and bit him with rows of teeth. No one heard his screams. I remember the first taste of his bloody, warm flesh in my mouth. The taste of iron, salt and skin. Little bits got stuck in between my teeth.

In case you are wondering, I've never been to the dentist in my life. Mom didn't want them to know what I was. But that didn't mean she wasn't obsessed with oral hygiene. Do you know how long it takes to brush the back rows of my teeth? How long it takes to floss? You'd think with a thousand teeth you wouldn't worry about losing one or two. Mom always says these teeth have to last me until I'm 120, so I better take care of them. Grandma made it to 120, and lost her teeth around then. It made it hard for her to feed and so she died early. I still miss her.

But I wasn't going to miss Anthony.

Finally feeling satiated, I pulled a pack of floss out of my backpack, carefully twisting the thread between the rows of my teeth. Anthony was my first taste of misogyny, and I will always remember him, the boy with the cloudy sky-blue eyes.

Last Dinner

THE TWO OF US ATE in near silence. Hesitantly, I took a small bite of pork tenderloin, and looked up at him, the man I married more than twenty years ago.

We were eating dinner when we got the news that the world was ending. It came with a phone call from my mother. I normally wouldn't answer the phone during a meal, but she rang three times, and I was worried it was an emergency. "What's wrong?" I asked her when I answered.

"The world is ending," she said.

"Oh, okay," I said. "We are eating dinner right now. Love you. Talk to you later."

I didn't believe her at first, but then the sirens sounded, and an alert blasted via text. The noise was jarring and trill like.

"What do you want to do?" I asked my husband. He was halfway through his pork and peas. He set down his fork.

"I suppose we should start saying our goodbyes."

"It's been a fun ride for the most part," he said, as the lights went out.

I reached for the candles and matches, striking them in the dark.

He pulled his chair to my side of the table and touched me on the arm. We hadn't been intimate in months. The touch felt strange, as though he was a stranger on the street bumping into me on accident.

"Do you want to call your lover and tell her goodbye?" I asked.

"I thought you didn't know," he said.

"A woman always knows," I said.

"Are you angry?" he asked.

"Yes, but I suppose it doesn't matter now in the grand scheme of things."

"I'm sorry. If it's any consolation, I wanted to grow old and die with you, not her. I chose you."

The sky outside our windows turned blood red.

"I wonder how much time we have left," I said.

I stood up and went to the window. He walked behind me and put his arms around me. I thought about shrugging them off but didn't. I took his hand and pulled him into the bedroom.

"Let's make love one last time," I said.

He took off his shirt and unzipped his pants. The fabric slid to the floor, coiled like a second set of snakeskin. He reached for me and took off my layers. I felt exposed under his gaze. He had hurt me more than once, but I still wanted him.

Mechanically, the pieces came together. Cold skin against cold skin, heated by friction. His fingers played me like an ensnared drum. A last moment of pleasure. He grinded into me and I felt the house tremble and shutter as the wind whipped outside. Out the window I could see the boards fly away, spinning into the distance. I could feel an eruption of explosive heat, as the roof was torn off. When the flames spread across the walls, we became one.

"At least you can't hurt me anymore," I whispered into his ear.

Headache

IGNORING ME AGAIN, she thought. And then it started.

The noise was unlike anything Josephine had ever heard. A hissing, whistling noise, with hot steam infiltrating her ear canals. She tried to sit down at the kitchen table, and covered her ears with her hands, burning the skin. Dizziness made the world spin around her. Her chair twisted out underneath her, and she landed on the floor. The black and white checked linoleum then danced beneath her, tossing and bucking her while she was on all fours.

The pressure on the insides of her head made her wonder if something had taken residence there and was about to bust out, like her skull was the shell of an egg, with whatever it was pecking strategically at the same spots trying to get it to crack. Right behind her left eye and the back of her skull at its base, alternating back and forth. Tremendous pressure and searing heat.

She tried to call for help. She knew her husband, Todd, was watching football in the living room. As always, he had the sound up high, on account of his hearing loss. She tried to call to him but the words came out in a gurgle. She crawled to the bathroom, praising God the door was open, clinging to the base of the sink and climbed up to get to the tap. She twisted the knob and the water flowed, snaking down cold on her singed hands. She wanted to get her head there, but struggled to pull up from the bucking ground. The pressure and heat continued to build. On the third try, with the last of her strength she managed to get her torso over the sink, bent down and placed her head under the stream of water. It didn't help the pressure like she thought it would.

Her skull made a popping sound, as it cracked, blood spattered across the mirror, and the creature finally crawled out, black speckled with silver and blood. It rinsed its wings under the water.

Josephine had about thirty seconds of consciousness—she watched the creature take its first flight and heard Todd cheering at the latest touchdown through what was left of her eardrums.

When Todd came in to use the bathroom. He thought she must have fallen and smacked her head on the sink. But that didn't explain the burns on Josephine's usually soft hands. He called 911. "I think my wife's head exploded," he said. He cradled one part of her skull, pushing it back into the other half like he could make her whole again. "Poor Josephine."

"Does she have a pulse?" the dispatcher asked.

"I'm not sure," he said, reaching for her pale, delicate wrist.

That was when he heard the growl behind him, and turned and saw the creature. Black insect eyes, a framework of wings unfolding beneath a silver-specked three-part body. Its black beak had a piece of flesh hanging off of it. It was the size of a sparrow but more bat-like in body.

Todd did wish he had a gun at that moment, not that it would have helped. He wished had a knife, but didn't dare unlock eyes with this creature. He weighed his options. Should he run to the kitchen and get one? There was no time. He bent slightly and grabbed a magazine from the rack and rolled it, maintaining eye contact. Carefully, moving slowly, he raised his arm. Then he swatted as hard as he could, hitting the creature. It gave a high-pitched shriek.

He dropped the cell phone in the toilet the moment the creature dive bombed his right eye socket, so the dispatcher couldn't hear his calls for help through the water. The beak dove straight into his brain, opening and closing, cutting his thoughts like scissors.

Bad English

WHEN KATHRYN'S SEVENTH GRADE English teacher tried to pull her onto his lap after school, she stabbed him in the dick with a pencil, it was the only thing she could find to use as a weapon and it wasn't very sharp but it did the job, unfortunately she wasn't a very good student and the principal didn't believe her when she told him what happened and while Mr. Morris declined to press charges out of "sheer embarrassment," he said, and Kathryn knew it was because he didn't want his wife to find out, and he was "forgiving" because the pencil didn't puncture his dick, but left it terribly bruised, and to this day Kathryn uses run-on sentences with sloppy punctuation and comma splices, and smiles when she does it, because she refused to learn to be a victim and the suspension and bad grammar were worth it.

Odd Couple

MELISSA CHECKED THE RSVPS on Facebook and set her laptop down on the kitchen counter, next to a mountain of unevenly cut salami, grapes and other hor d'oeuvres on a silver tray. They'd polished the platter just for the occasion, and it still had a little tarnish at the edges. "Crap, I'm not even sure anybody's coming to the party," she said. "I'm so sorry, honey."

Brian shrugged. "Turning forty isn't as big of a deal as it used to be."

She ducked into the powder room to reapply her makeup and hide the worry on her face. She stopped herself from telling him he needed more friends. It was not the time. But people with good friends live longer, happier lives, she thought. What if I get hit by a bus and he has no one? They'd only been together for a year. He'd survive, but somehow, she still worried.

Melissa blotted her red lipstick with a piece of toilet paper and tossed it in the trash can. The lid made a loud, metal noise when it slammed shut, almost like a gong.

The doorbell rang and Bruce, the neighbor with silvery hair, stood on the doorstep. The party was supposed to have started an hour ago, and he was the first one to arrive. Or rather the only one to arrive.

"Sorry, I'm late…" His voice trailed off as he looked around the spotless room with the empty chairs. "I brought you this. Happy birthday." He handed Brian a bottle of champagne. "Where is everybody?"

"Would you like anything to drink?" Melissa asked, taking his brown, wool coat and placing it on the rack. They had cleared the rack before to make sure there was room for everyone's coats. His brown coat hung lonely on the wooden pegs.

The three of them headed to the food in the kitchen and Melissa began stress eating salami, popping piece after salty piece into her mouth and smearing her lipstick on her teeth. Bruce ate a couple cheese curds and glanced over at the sheet of cake perched on the coffee table. Brian's picture was on it, and "Happy Birthday, Brian" was written in frosting. Brian's brown hair looked perfect, and his eyes shone in the edible photo. It was one of the first ones that Melissa had ever taken of him, on a hike in the mountains.

"So I take it, you two aren't football fans then?" Bruce stuttered in surprise. "You don't have the game on?"

Brian's face bloomed red. "Was there a game today? Is that why no one's here?"

"I can only stay for halftime, actually," Bruce said after a pause. "Just meant to stop by."

"Personally, I think the game is a bit barbaric," Melissa blurted out. "With all those head injuries. I don't like to exploit other people's pain for my entertainment."

Bruce's smile receded.

"I'm sorry. I didn't mean to knock something you love," she added. She shrunk back against the wall.

"I can see why you two don't have many friends," Bruce said, heading to the coat rack. "And those players aren't exploited. They make millions."

As Bruce walked out, Brian yelled out after him, "thanks for coming!" He turned to Melissa. "Well, that was awkward."

Melissa started to tear up. "I just wanted you to have a happy birthday, to have some friends. I'm sorry I messed it all up. I always say the wrong thing."

"It wasn't your fault. I blame my mother for having me on a Super Bowl Sunday," he said. "It happens now and then with the date."

He put his arm around Melissa and pulled her to the couch. "I think we are the only two people in the world who don't like football."

"Did you know all along the game was today?" she asked.

"Honey, I've told you, I don't really like many other people, just you. As an introvert, I'm relieved no one else came."

The sheet cake took up the expanse of the coffee table. His over-sized picture stared at them.

"You look good on this cake," she said. "Still so young. Still so appetizing."

"This is the youngest I'll ever be," he said. "Would you like some?" He grinned while cutting her a slice of his face. "It'll make you feel better."

The Wall

MY MICKEY MOUSE watch is ruined. It's not the right time, and its face is cloudy with trapped moisture. Mickey's hands point in the wrong direction. Ever since we fled the city, time has become meaningless.

It's strange that people flee cities during disasters, thinking they are safer elsewhere, but they always end up in traffic jams. There was no running from this war, but we didn't know that. When the lights went off and the tornado sirens blasted, we took our tent and our car, a cooler, a camping stove, an old rifle that had been in the family for fifty years. We had bullets but no idea how to use the thing or whether it even worked. Boots and coats, came along for the ride, even though it wasn't that season, because, "we don't know what the future will hold," Dad said. Dad let me bring a backpack with toys. I couldn't bear to leave my favorite stuffed frog behind. I've kissed him a thousand times, so much that the fuzz has worn off his mouth, but he has yet to turn into a prince.

We've been trying to make it into Mexico for the last seventeen days. We drove to the border and ran out of gas, waiting in line behind tens of thousands of other cars. The Mexican government has imposed limits on refugees. It seems spiteful, a holdover from days when Mexicans had to sneak into the U.S. illegally. Can you imagine people wanting to come to the United States? I asked Dad why we didn't try Canada, and he said it was because they were under attack as well. The wall that was built fifteen years ago to keep Mexicans out of the U.S., had become a barrier to our entry into Mexico.

"Politicians are so short sighted," my dad said.

My dad is pacing around outside the car right now. Mom is crying in the back seat. My little brother is asleep. He's gotten used to sleeping upright. I haven't. We are tired and thirsty. Some Mexican church members, missionaries, brought us water, but we use it sparingly. I hate going to the bathroom at the side of the road. I'm afraid of being separated from my family.

The missionaries are back, and they ask my parents if they can take my brother and I— they have space in their trunk and don't get stopped at the checkpoints.

"They'll be safe with us and when you make it into the country, you will be reunited," a nun says.

My father has always been wary of organized religion, but he nods. "How many children have you smuggled across the border?"

"Fifty-four so far," the nun says. She lifts my brother from his seat and wraps his arms around her neck. I eye her warily.

"What about my parents?" I ask.

"They will come in time," the nun says. I want to believe her. I tell myself to believe her. I'm afraid to stay in this dead car on this dead road, and I'm afraid of the ashes I saw from the city, the fires and smoke in the distance. I am afraid of starving and dying of thirst. I am afraid of breathing poisonous gas. I can taste it in the air, but it hasn't killed me yet. But I am also afraid to leave my parents. I'm not sure what is the most terrifying.

"You must be very quiet," the nun says. My brother is awake now, bewildered in her arms. He is not a fan of strangers generally, but these are strange times.

I kiss my father and mother good-bye. I taste her cheek, wet with tears. I have never been an overly affectionate kid. I don't like to kiss people, but this is different.

"Why are you crying," I ask.

"Because I'm happy," she says. "You will at least be safe." I know she's lying about being happy, trying to be brave. I'm old enough to know that.

My mother is a teacher. Her whole class is probably gone. The school district she worked in was an hour west of our house, much closer to the strike zone.

"We will find a way over the wall, I promise," my dad says. I want to believe him too. He's a carpenter. Maybe he can build something to get over the wall, or dig under. I wonder what he's got to work with. Not much.

It's dark in the trunk, pitch black and stuffy. My little brother sobs when he's put in there. I can feel his tears with my hands. I wipe them, and gently stroke the side of his face, and he quiets, but his chest continues to heave. The interior of the trunk is a coarse fabric, dusty. I run my fingers over the sides. I'm not sure why. It only heightens my terror. The engine starts, and I can taste the gasoline in the air.

I hit the light on my watch. Other kids got mobile phones or tablets, I got a stinking watch. Of course, now that the networks are gone, they are just blocks of plastic and glass. The tiny light flips on, illuminating Mickey's face. It calms me. I hit it periodically. I watch the second-hand move, the minute hand, the hour hand.

When we arrive, the trunk opens. We are ushered into a crowded room where the missionaries feed us soup and give us blankets. There is a hole in the ceiling. I wonder if it was made from a bomb, but then remember that the war hasn't hit here yet. I can see the moon, so bright and silver like a coin.

And I know. Even before I hear the bombs in the distance, I know.

Otis Boy

MILA DROVE THE RED CAMARO down a deserted highway lined with dirty blond wild grass and open sky, kissed by foothills at the horizon. Her purple headscarf, covered in planet and moon symbols fluttered behind her. Smiling softly, thinking of a new beginning in New Mexico, without her boyfriend, Charles, Mila could see a happy future ahead. Her ankle shifted and her foot pressed the gas pedal a little harder. There was no one on this road but her, and she felt the thrill of driving with a strong engine, the speed tossing her head back like an uncontrollable laugh.

Her only regret was leaving her rescue "teacup" pig behind, but at a whopping 500-plus pounds, Otis was a bit much to cram into a coupe, and the battery in Mila's truck had died at the worst possible moment.

She had begged her friend Jessie bring Otis to her ranch in her truck, and she had agreed. "Please try to bring his Frisbee and his blue baby blanket, if you can," she had told Jessie, "He will come when you call him. You just have to yell out, Otis boy."

Charles had never let Mila drive his Camaro before, and he certainly never intended to let her take it with her when she left. But her earnings as a tarot card reader and astrologer had helped pay for his hot rod ride. Mila knew she shouldn't feel guilty about taking the car… She sped down the rural highway on her way to her New Mexico life.

It was a sad thought, but maybe Otis was the love of her life. Even coming straight from the rescue and despite being an animal, he had better manners than Charles and his grunts were more meaningful. Charles, who called her profession stupid, who disrespected the planets, and the power of the moon. Charles, who didn't understand her past trauma. Charles, who yelled at her, but always stopped just short of hitting her with his fists.

"The cards show there is no future for us," she had told him when she left. He had torn the cards up and thrown the pieces in her face.

When the sirens started flashing, Mila's first inclination was to increase speed, but she dutifully pulled over. Her hands shook on the wheel, and she told herself she had broken no laws.

"Was I speeding, Officer?" she asked when the trooper walked up to her window. "I didn't think I was."

"No, this car was reported stolen. License and registration."

She fumbled through the glove box and pulled them out. "I'm on the registration," she said.

"Indeed, you are," he said, looking at the paper. "Was there some kind of misunderstanding between you and your partner?"

"Actually, I'm leaving my boyfriend, and we bought this car together…" she added.

The trooper nodded and tipped his hat. "Be careful pulling out," he said. "I thought this call was the weirdest thing. I'm not surprised there's some funny business about it."

"Why is that?" Mila asked.

"Because the man who reported it said something odd."
"What was that?" Mila's heart rate quickened.
"He said if we caught the thief to tell them something."
"Tell them what?" Mila's mouth went dry.
"That he was making bacon."

Red Dedication

I MET NATE FIVE YEARS AGO at a writers' workshop at the public library. That should have been a red flag. All writers are crazy, you know. What drives a writer to spend hours a day staring at a blank page and filling it with characters, letters, words, monstrous dreams? Usually some kind of flirtation with insanity, a disconnect from reality? I should know.

He asked me if I wanted to grab coffee and we could write for a while too. It seemed innocent enough. But like an artist, he used me as his muse. He started writing a character named Delilah who looked like me. Blond, green eyed with round, pert breasts and muted makeup other than red lipstick. Her favorite color was red, like mine. Red sweaters. Red dresses. She sobbed listening to the same songs through her earbuds, even in public, loved to write in coffee shops and had bad choice in men. That part was actually pretty cliché but unfortunately for me, true.

We were like kindred spirits. At the time, I thought twin souls. He never asked me out. He never let me read his whole novel either. "It's not ready," he'd say. "I'm not ready." He'd look down at his hands. It took years for him to create. Just snippets. Tiny pieces of a life he created, a life that oddly mirrored my own. Then he took years querying agents, until one day he told me it was going to be published. We celebrated by writing at our coffee shop, typing on laptops next to each other for hours. More years passed. He griped about the editing process in his soft-spoken way, said he didn't want to stray from his vision of who Delilah was, but there was so much pressure to make her something different.

"I couldn't do anything about it," he said. "I gave up my creative control when I signed the contract. Editors." He shrugged.

Even so, I felt a pang of jealousy when he talked about his publisher. For I had yet to finish my pirate fantasy novels, the series that stretched from one century to another.

When his book came out, I looked for my name in the acknowledgments and didn't find it. But he did sign me a copy. At his book launch, I held the paperback in my hands and waited in line like everyone else. My writing buddy, my friend was a success. I wasn't particularly bitter. Eagerly, I took the book home and started reading about Delilah in bed. The stalking was creepy, but it was the assault that made me gag. I wanted to put the book down and turn off the light, but I couldn't. I was horrified to see the way he handled her, to see what happened next. It's not me, I told myself. But it was. I could feel the cloth wadded up in my mouth and Delilah's heart pounding in my ears. In the end, I could feel the sting of the knife against her throat, cold and sharp. The police weren't coming. It was up to her to fight back, and she couldn't do it. Tears streamed down my face, as the knife cut deeper into my flesh. Reaching up, I felt the blood, slippery crimson streaking through my hands.

Because I was Delilah and Nate was a killer, not just a writer. He had control over life and death in the world he created. I dropped the book, my hands shaking and reminded myself it wasn't real, that I was being crazy, like all writers are crazy. I couldn't finish reading the pages. Was he a writer or a magician? Because I know I felt that knife against my throat.

The next day, Nate sent me a text asking me how I liked the book. I didn't answer. And the next time he asked me to meet up at a coffee shop, I didn't come. I did not want to be written into any more of his stories, thinly veiled or otherwise, or die in his pages again.

But it was curiosity that made me pick up the phone when he called in the end.

"Did you see I dedicated the book to you?" he asked. "Did that weird you out?"

"You killed me," I said. "I'm a human being, not material."

"The editor wanted that to happen, not me. I had no control," he said.

"You're spineless, Nate. And messed up."

"It wasn't about you. It wasn't you."

"Oh, so now you deny it."

"Forgive me? I'll buy you a coffee."

I wavered. Because he was my friend. Because there was a murderous edge to his voice.

Grandma

IT'S LIKE A HORROR FILM. I'm only thirty years old, but one random morning, I have changed into my grandmother overnight. After few steps out of my bed, at first, I barely notice. I can tell my posture is off as I hobble my way to the bathroom. I feel shorter. I go to brush my teeth, and I drop the toothbrush on the floor when I look in the mirror. There she is, my grandmother, staring back at me. Her wrinkled face has a certain amount of charm, I admit—her white, billowy hair and faded blue gray eyes. I touch the rough skin on my face. I tug on one of my ear lobes. It has gotten longer. My breasts have too. As I reach down to pick my toothbrush off the tile floor, they hang long and tube-like from my chest, so much lower than they used to.

In a panic, I run back into my bedroom, taking short, quick breaths and grab my cell phone off the nightstand. I call my doctor's office as fast as I can, my hands shaking as I punch in the numbers.

"It's Mary Nelson," I say. "I need to see Dr. Williams right away."

"What's the health issue?" the receptionist asks. "Have you traveled to West Africa recently?"

"It's not Ebola," I say, my voice trembling old lady like. "I don't know what it is, but it's definitely not Ebola."

"Ok, ma'am, but what's wrong exactly?"

"I seem to have aged fifty years overnight," I say. "I'm feeling frail, not like myself."

"Ok, then," the receptionist says in an unsure voice that makes me doubt she believes me. "Well, I've got you down for two p.m."

I go into the kitchen and open the fridge. It's harder to open than it used to be. My bicep muscles have gone slack. What's left of my triceps now hang loosely with sagging skin dangling from my arms. I pull out a carton of eggs and start boiling three of them. The pot of water is so heavy, it takes me two hands to lift it. I time the eggs for exactly ten minutes, toss them in cold water and then crack and eat them at the kitchen table. As I'm swallowing a soft, orange yolk I realize that this was what she ate for breakfast every day, my grandmother. Then I start to crave a glass of red wine. Strange, she was an alcoholic. Granted, she hid it well, I think, but really grandma? It's not even noon.

I wander into the living room and pull out a photo album with her in it. I look at the picture and walk over to the hallway mirror. I glance at the photo and my reflection. There are my new eyes, her old eyes looking back at me. There's my new, old mouth… granted it's a little more weathered with time. Is it just a resemblance, or am I really her?

I decide to get dressed. That should be easy enough, except none of my clothes fit me anymore. My grandmother had a body like an egg with skinny little legs underneath a rounder torso, and so do I now. I pull on my favorite purple sweater. It is too short, doesn't even cover my rounded belly. I put on a yellow T-shirt; it mashes my boobs into weird shapes, like two over-ripened pieces of fruit. My mostly fit thirty-year-old body is gone. And the funny thing is my pants are too loose. It's like the weight has been redistributed in odd places. I stand in front of the mirror, staring in horror and disbelief. I put the sweater back on, pulling it down periodically, trying to stretch it out, but I can feel it riding up.

I go back into my room, lay down on the bed, and I think about her. What would she have done? She would have locked herself in her room drinking. That's an option, I guess. But no. I don't want to do that, not yet.

Danny, my boyfriend, can always tell when I'm having a bad day. Like some kind of psychic, he calls. "Hey babe, you want to meet for lunch?" he asks.

"Not today," I say, my voice shaking. I don't want him to see me like this. He loves me but does he love me enough to date me as a senior citizen? "I'm not feeling well," I say.

"Okay, I'll stop by after work and bring you some soup or something," he says.

"No, that's okay. I don't want you to catch this, whatever this is," I say. "Thanks though."

Once I hang up, I decide I can't wait until two p.m. I have to see Dr. Williams immediately. I put on my jacket, my floppy sun hat and a pair of large sunglasses. I don't want anyone else to see me like this.

I get in my car, slump in the driver's seat and adjust the rearview mirror lower to adjust for my shrunken height. I catch a glimpse of myself in the mirror and rummage through my purse. I apply some lipstick, smear my lips unevenly with a deep red. It can't hurt, I think sheepishly. I have to keep trying to look my best. My thoughts race, but the drive is slow. I'm not sure why but I can't seem to push my foot down hard enough on the gas pedal to go past twenty miles per hour. It takes me ages to parallel park. Twisting my tight neck to look back behind the car, I hear a crack. It startles me to realize my body made that sound. Then I hear another sound—a thwack noise from the car behind me, as I hit it with my bumper. I pull forward a few inches and get out.

"Oh my," I say out loud, as I inspect the damage. "Gosh darn." I even talk like her, I realize. For a moment, I ponder if I should leave a note. Squinting more closely, I convince myself that surely that scratch was there before. Besides, it's barely noticeable. Or maybe it is noticeable. Is my vision blurry? Grandma always did wear glasses. I squint harder, quickly scribble a note with my information and an apology and leave it on the windshield. Paying the bill is the least of my worries at this moment.

I walk into the doctor's office. I sit in one of those uncomfortable chairs, fumble through a stack of magazines on the table next to me. I stare at the super models in the glossy pages. Their skin is so young looking, so firm. I touch my sagging cheeks with my fingers.

"Hmm," Dr. Williams says when he sees me. "To be honest, I barely recognized you."

"What do you think the problem is, doctor?" I ask. He presses the cold, round part of his stethoscope against the wrinkled skin of my chest and listens to my heart pound.

"You know, this really isn't my area of expertise," he says. "Your vitals are fine. You aren't running a temperature. You appear healthy. I think you'd be better off seeing a dermatologist."

"A dermatologist?" I say, my voice getting loud. "You've got to be kidding."

"What kind of moisturizer do you use?" he says. "Just out of curiosity."

"I don't use any moisturizer," I say.

"Well, maybe that's your problem," he says.

"Doctor, I don't think you are taking this seriously enough," I say, my voice rising an octave. "Can't you at least run some blood tests to find out what's going on? For the love of Pete!" I cringe as I hear her words come out of my mouth.

He sends me to the lab where the nurse gives me a quizzical look after glancing at my chart. "Is this date of birth correct?" she asks. "And your insurance information?" I'm not sure which one she is more concerned with. I look away as she takes vials and vials of my bright red blood from a blue protruding vein at the inside of my elbow. "Dr. Williams will call you sometime next week with the results," she says, smiling. She tapes on the cotton ball and pats me on the arm. Is that supposed to be reassuring? I wonder.

I leave the office with a referral to a dermatologist but the next appointment isn't available for two months. Two months. I cry in my car, bow my head against the steering wheel and sob like a little girl. No, there's got to be something I can do about this, I think, so I drive slowly to the pharmacy. I buy some "age defying" moisturizer and slather it on my face as soon as I get back into the car.

When I pull up to my house, there's Danny waiting for me at the door. I walk up to him and he puts an arm around me. "You didn't sound right on the phone," he says. "I thought I'd come over and check on you."

"But Danny, look at me," I say, taking off my sunglasses and whipping off my hat. "I'm not all right. I'm so old." I've given up, I think. I am going to go inside, shut the door and start drinking red wine immediately.

"Mary, whatever this is, we'll deal with it together." He pushes back a wisp of my white, billowy hair, behind my ear.

"Can you deal with this?" I say, pulling down my V-neck sweater showing off my stretched out, wrinkled boobs. One of them has fallen out of my bra, sinking lower than the other.

He pauses for a moment, then looks me in the eye as he grips my shoulders.

"Mary, your appearance doesn't matter. Your physique doesn't matter," he says. "It doesn't matter. I love you, and I want to be old with you."

"Really?" I say.

"Really," he says.

And just like that, I am thirty again.

Eyes Like a Prison

THELMA SAT STRAIGHT with almost impossible posture as she sat down in the auditorium. When Steven joined her, she stiffened in her folding chair even more and turned slightly away from him. From a distance, it looked like she was ignoring him at first, but then the two murmured in low voices together. "They all look so cute up there in their tutus," she said. "I always wanted to do ballet as a child."

She asked Steven which girl was his, and he pointed to the little, freckled, white girl to the right. Thelma pointed out Vanessa on the left, even though it was obvious who her daughter was, the only black girl on stage.

"You remember me?" Steven asked. "We used to play together as kids."

She nodded slowly and said his name, "Steven Adam Goodwin. We used to play baseball in the park… before your parents… oh, nevermind."

Thelma turned to face him, her face cheering with friendly recognition. They smiled at each other for a moment before he ruined everything.

"Anyone ever tell you your eyes are like a prison?" he asked.

"What's that supposed to mean?" She furrowed her brow in confusion. Was that supposed to be some kind of weird pickup line at a recital, she wondered.

"You are so beautiful you could destroy a man's life," he slurred.

Unflinching, she locked eyes with him directly. "Aren't you married, Mr. Goodwin? Where's your wife? Have you been drinking?"

"Just a little," he said. "She wasn't feeling well, so she stayed home. Where's your husband?" Something in his tone implied that she never had one.

"Where he's been for four years. In a casket at the Craw Hill Cemetery, thank you for asking." The words came out extra cold.

"Forgive me," he said. "It's just you were my first love. Love makes men stupid."

"Don't I know it," she muttered.

His hand was on the folding chair next to her, inches from her hand. There was a time when she would have loved to take his hand in hers many years ago. But that time had passed. She took a good look at Steven Goodwin, the rough stubble dotting his face, the worn lines around his mouth from smoking, his tired, bloodshot still sky-blue eyes.

He started to lean forward and sideways toward her, like he was going to whisper something profane in her ear, but she stopped him, putting up her hand.

"Knock it off, Steven Goodwin," she said in a low warning tone. "The show is starting." She scooted her chair away from him as quietly as she could.

As the little girls twirled on stage, little Vanessa saw her mother's unhappy expression and thought she had done something wrong. During a direction change, she went the opposite way, accidentally slamming the freckled girl hard, who in turn bumped another child, causing her to fall. Thelma was never certain that Mr. Goodwin had a broken heart that night. But whatever it was had cascaded through the recital. The fallen child wailed, tears streaming down her chubby cheeks. The girl had a fractured ankle, as well as some surprisingly sophisticated cuss words for a kindergartener.

In a Serial Killer's Garden

THE PROBLEM WITH DISSOLVING A BODY in acid is that it's bad for the environment, Rachel thought as she read the news that day. She wrinkled her nose in disgust at the latest story about a murderer who did just that. Talk about ecologically irresponsible. It was much better to burn the bodies and use the ash in her garden. Rachel had a keen interest in other murderers and read about their methods, carefully to avoid the mistakes that got them caught.

Victim number one was pushing daisies. Rachel looked out her window and remembered her old landlady and the circular glasses that used to slip down her nose. She kept them as a souvenir on the windowsill. The last trace of the woman. Now Rachel lived rent-free.

This house was her house. The garden was her garden. The daisies were hers. She sighed contently and took a slow slurp of her hot coffee. Her flower garden was the perfect resting place, tranquil. Her kiln out back was eight feet long and could get to 1,900 degrees Fahrenheit. Her nearest neighbors were thirteen miles away. There were advantages to country living. Rachel enjoyed baking bread and pies, and leaving them on the wide windowsill, cooling next to the glasses.

Her latest victim, Rick, was in the basement, tied up and knocked unconscious. She'd tend to him at nightfall. Right now, was time to tend to the flowers.

Different clusters of flowers, each representing a victim swayed in streaks of color across the yard.

Roses for Roy

Sweet peas for Patrick

Daisies for Delilah

Tulips for Todd

Fire lilies for Linda

Black-eyed Susans for Susan

Geraniums for George

Snapdragons for Samantha

Hydrangeas for Henry

Roy was an ex-boyfriend who made the mistake of calling Rachel a giant freak and telling her no one else would ever love a woman as large or ugly as she was. Rachel was over six feet and outweighed him by forty pounds. Delilah was the landlady, of course. Other than that, she had no true personal connections with her victims.

Rachel worked for streets and sanitation, collecting recycling. Patrick, Linda, George, Samantha and Henry, had all mixed their recyclables. Todd and Susan, they didn't recycle at all, dumping their plastic milk containers and old papers directly into the trash. Rick had thrown out a perfectly good couch on a rainy day.

Rachel tossed her coffee grounds into the compost pile. She pulled her long blond hair into a ponytail, put on her muddy gardening gloves and grabbed the garden hoe outside the back door.

The soil around the roses was rich, and the fight against weeds was always a battle. Something about Roy and his ashes brought out both the beauty and ugliness in the world. Rachel pulled out the roots, abandoning the gloves, so she could feel them with her fingers, pulling them up without snapping them in half with remnants in the ground. A thistle had popped up in Patrick's section, one of the most stubborn weeds. She put the gloves back on and started to dig with her shovel. Removed most of it. She didn't own any pesticides, but sprayed the roots with white vinegar. When she got to the daisies, a strange red bug caught her eye. She got down to the ground and was watching its antennae twitch, trying to identify whether it was friend or foe to the plants, when the hoe slammed down on her head. "What the hell?" she yelled.

"Ahh, Rick," she mumbled.

"Who are you and how do you know my name and what are you trying to do to me?" Rick's wrists were bloody from where the ties had cut into his skin.

"How did you get out of the basement?" she asked.

He hit her with the hoe again, and she saw flashes of color behind her eyes. Warm, sticky blood ran down her face. She wiped it from her mouth.

"Your name, it's on your statement." She gasped. "Why on Earth did you put a perfectly good couch out on the street in the rain?"

"Bedbugs." He hit her again. "Give me your phone."

"I'm not a fan of most bugs either." She looked back down at the red bug. "Sorry I misjudged you," she said. She stumbled to her feet. "I don't have a phone."

"You've got to be fucking kidding me," Rick said. He went to hit her again, but this time, Rachel grabbed the handle of the hoe with all the force she could muster, just under the metal.

"The nice thing about working for the department of streets and sanitation is that it makes you strong," Rachel said, smiling. She twisted the tool, her blood making the handle slippery. Rick stumbled back, and she wrenched it from his hands.

"What's your favorite flower?" she asked.

Star Slut

I LOOK AT THE STARS OUTSIDE of my starship's window. If only I could pack them in my suitcase and take them with me. The engines hum, a soft, sad song to my ears.

It was a long, lonely road to starship captain. I can't tell you how many people I had to screw to get to the top. Which hasn't helped my personal relationships over the years. It's crazy that monogamy is still so highly prized in the galaxy considering birth control has been around for hundreds of years and they've eradicated all STDs. Jealousy lacks a cure—it's human nature, that desire to control your partner and who they sleep with and how they love or don't. But I digress. At least I had fun with it. My nickname was Star Slut in the academy.

They fired me for insubordination against the admiral. I used to have dreams about cleaning out my desk. But how do you clean out a room on a starship? There are trinkets from other planets. I have a rock collection that is out of this world. There is no room for it in the cargo hold. No box strong enough to carry its weight on earth. All those stones will have to be left on board.

Boyle, my former first mate and my replacement knocks on my door. He's a Brefeeking, with golden skin that shimmers under the light. He had always been a good lover and friend, from my days back in the academy.

"Would you have done it? Would you have terraformed the planet?" I ask. I don't turn. I don't look at him or his black eyes.

"Yes, yes I would have," he says. "You know that."

"Even though it destroys the existing life on that world? Destroys the native atmosphere, kills millions of life-forms?"

"We ruled out intelligent life on that planet." Boyle sighs. "All the specimens tested came back negative, and we tested most of the life-forms we found."

"Does life only have value if it's intelligent? What if we missed something?"

"Next you are going to tell me you've gone vegan," he says.

"Maybe I have." I fold my captain's uniform and start to toss it into my suitcase, but then realize I can't wear it anymore, anyway. I throw the garment against the gray wall of the ship and start crying. This life is all I've known for the last fifteen years.

He puts an arm around my shoulders, and I shrug it off.

"Fuck off, Boyle," I say. "How many people did you have to sleep with to get to the top?"

"I got here on my own merit," he says. Then we both burst out laughing at the ridiculousness of that statement.

"I'll miss you, Boyle," I say.

"I'll miss you, too," he says. "I admire your conviction."

"Do you," I ask. It was more of a statement than a question. "But not enough to follow it."

"No, not enough to follow it," he says. "The process has already started."

I look down at the planet outside the window, it has rotated into view. A sliver of orange light has outlined the edge of its surface. In a flash, it will be completely different, transformed.

Decimated, annihilated. Destroyed. Like me.

Letting Go

TAYLOR SURVEYED THE SCENE, her parent's house, the things they left behind after the accident. Absent-mindedly, she fingered the crimson and blue marks on her neck. She moved her head around. You'd almost think she had been in the car with them, she thought. What would her mother have thought if she knew what Harry had done? Taylor sobbed as she filled a cardboard box full of her mother's books, taking them out of the old, blue chest one by one. Her mother always said these books she kept were like old friends, ones worth visiting time and time again. Some were signed first editions. The wooden chest was flung open, its top a gaping blue mouth that threatened to swallow her whole.

The chest has the initials of family names from her great-grandmother's side generations ago and the date 1800 painted on in light blue. Overall, its body was a dark, faded blue with flowers painted on the front. Black iron handles hung heavy at its sides, and a large iron key was wedged in the lock. There were scrapes too, where the wood met wood, and bits of paint had broken off.

Dozens of people had held its handles. So many generations that they lost count. The chest started out as a wedding gift two hundred and fifty years ago. A father for his daughter fitted the pieces of wood together. The couple filled it with heirlooms nestled in linens at the foot of their wedding bed. Eventually, after a generation or two, it became mundane. It went out of style and was moved into a barn. Filled with tools, buried under bales of hay, it was forgotten then found in the nineteen fifties when the farm was sold. Unexpectedly still beautiful, it was shipped to a little house in Copenhagen with a tag telling the address that was still tied in string. The chest lived with a couple, her great-grandparents, whose son moved to America. They filled it with pictures from Victorian times to the Depression through WWII. When they died, their son emptied it, keeping the photos, and sent it to her mother, shipped it in a container across the ocean, then it was sent across America, from house to house with her parents.

Taylor knew Harry would never let her keep it.

She could hear him breathing behind her. He'd followed her to the house. Why hadn't she remembered to lock the door?

"You're here," she said.

Harry crouched down and gave Taylor an awkward hug, where she sat on the floor. She flinched reflexively, as if he were going to hurt her again.

"Don't worry," he said, softly. "We have a week to figure this all out. We can figure it out together. I'm here for you. I'll always be here for you."

"What am I going to do with all this stuff?" she said, sniffling. "We don't have room for all this stuff in our apartment, and the things I do want to keep, I'm not sure what to do with them."

"Like what?" Harry said, frowning. "What would you want to keep out of all this crap?"

"What about this chest?" she asked. "Look at the date on the front of this thing. It's been in my family for over two hundred and fifty years. That means something, doesn't it?"

"It means your family is a bit compulsive about keeping things," he said. "Maybe it's time to let go."

"Let go," she said, pausing. "Harry, maybe it's time to let you go."

She wiped her eyes, then pulled out her mother's gun from the cardboard box. It was another thing she'd found in the chest. Through the tears, she was imagining all the room in her apartment if she got rid of her abusive boyfriend, room for old books, and room for better loves. It was time. She had the crimson and purple marks on her neck to prove it.

"Get in the chest," she said, standing up and pointing the gun at his head. He stepped in, one foot at a time, with his hands raised over his head. Then he curled up in the fetal position, protecting his head with his hands. She slammed the top of the chest back down over him, turned the oversized iron key in the lock and pulled it out.

"Let me out, right now, or I'll fucking kill you," he screamed. His voice was muffled but she could make out every word.

"Like hell, I will," she said.

As the hours and noise passed, Taylor thought about taking the books and setting the chest on fire. She bet the old wood would burn well. But in the end, she hired movers to take it to the storage locker the next day. Never telling them what was inside. It was contained, pretty much airtight, the perfect vessel to carry her abusive boyfriend from this life to the next. Suffocation was simpler than a bullet.

And Harry was right about one thing. It was time to let the old chest go.

The Day Time Melted

THE DAY TIME MELTED, I was standing in the kitchen, stirring a pot of boiling water, making chai.

The ginger, cardamom, and cloves swirled in the water. Steam rose hot, and I smelled their aroma. The peppercorn hadn't yet made it in.

The day time melted, I hadn't yet heard the news. The bombs had not hit and exploded. I never knew they were coming. The government hadn't known how to stop the bombs, but the scientists had found a way to stop time. They just didn't realize how dangerous it was.

So the bombs hovered while the world stopped.

Light became brighter. Blinding yellow light. At first, some thought it was the bombs. But it had something to do with time, the speed of light. Light stopping in its tracks. Growing illumination.

As the bright yellow immersed me, I wanted to tell my husband I loved him, but he wasn't in the room. Stuck with warm spices of chai, in one moment forever hovering, spoon in hand, the loving light brightened and engulfed me. I felt myself evaporate like steam, the day time melted.

Murder Cabin

IT WAS CLEAR THAT SOMEONE or something had died here when I first walked past the threshold of the cabin. The wood was stained in an irregular pattern in the middle of the room. Instead of imagining the body falling to the ground, I imagined pleasant shapes like I was looking at a cloud drifting over me in the sky. *Did that part of the blood look like a unicorn?* Years of writing about crime, violence, and tragedy had made blood seem like a normal part of life. I was looking forward to retiring in the mountains and living peacefully. But even so, I wondered if I could live with the stain.

"I'm not sure if I can see myself living here," I said.

The Realtor, a petite, blonde dressed in a skirt and heels, kicked at the rug on the floor, hiding part of the stain with its frayed edges, as though erasing it with her toe. I imagined her in a swimsuit, testing to see if the water was warm. Then I imagined her without the suit and felt a pang of annoyance at myself because I wasn't looking for anything right now, especially not with my Realtor. *Women like her always cause trouble. No, that's not fair. I'm trouble, and I missed my deadline on relationships.* It was a lie I had told myself so many times, I believed it.

I refocused on the stain. From another angle, it looked like a bulldog, I noted. "Interesting," I said.

I pulled back the plaid, thread-bare curtain on the window, then let the dusty fabric fall back over it. I turned and pointed at the ax in the corner. "Was that the murder weapon?"

The Realtor cleared her throat. "No, no," she said. "It was a shot-gun." The words came out hesitantly, but firmly.

She was known for her honesty, inside the real estate community and out, and had great reviews online. Then again, reviews can be faked. *If your mother says she loves you, check it out…* as I had told my students in journalism school.

"I was wondering why the list price was so low," I said. During years of covering crime, I had never written a story on murder impact-ing real estate prices.

I imagined putting my grandfather's old Remington typewriter in the corner and writing poetry about wildflowers. Outside, amongst the aspens with their fluttering green mirror-like leaves, it was serene. The crisp smell of nature, the caress of wind blowing through, were a welcome change from the constant adrenaline of deadlines and police crime scene tape. But how peaceful was it here really? *Crime happens everywhere.*

"It's definitely below the rest of the marketplace in this area," she said. "It's a bargain. You won't find another place like this again."

"Is it haunted?" I asked.

"No, you have to bring your own ghost," she said, with an uneasy smile. "There have been no complaints. What do you think?"

"It does take a little imagination," I say. I looked at the log walls of the one-room cabin, the green appliances, and the grime on an old cast-iron stove. I noted the dull finish on the floorboards, but with a little sanding and finishing, maybe they could shine again.

"I don't think that stain is going to come out," I muttered.

"It's a conversation starter, maybe?" the Realtor said.

"There's no electricity is there," I add. "And I see there's an outhouse."

"You can buy the property as a tear down, if you like. Keep the cabin or demolish it. The choice is yours. You strike me as the rugged type."

I snorted at that. "Who was murdered here?"

"It actually wasn't murder," the Realtor said, glancing down at the stain. "It was suicide."

"In some languages and cultures, they call that self-murder, if you want to get technical, I guess," I said. "Well, that explains why I didn't hear about it. The papers don't report on suicides around here, unless they take place in a public space."

"How do you know that?" she asked.

"Oh, I'm a retired journalist, and I read everything, and I keep every paper. I was one of the few left in the newsroom before I took the retirement package."

"Well, you'll be able to start a fire with all those old newspapers then," she added. "They'll finally be good for something."

She stared out the window, her gaze soft and dream-like. "I've never really cared for the media," she said. "The media is the worst."

"Not to be a spoilsport, but the media are actually plural," I said without missing a beat. "And ignorance is the worst."

She gave me a look that was measuredly neutral. A smirk and eyes that were cool at the corners, not quite smiling. She was a strange Realtor, I thought. You'd think she'd be trying to flatter me.

"Is it still a biohazard?" I knelt down and touched the discolored wood with my hand. I expected it to be sticky, but the floor was mostly smooth to the touch.

"Nah, I don't think so," she said.

"Isn't it hard to shoot yourself with a shotgun?" I turned my head up toward her and caught the ax on the back of it. I heard the thud and split in my skull and the vibration of impact in my jaw. I slumped forward and watched the stain spread on the floor. Maybe she's not so honest after all. So much for a so-called suicide.

"I hate the media," she repeated, her voice tinny and distant. "The media is the worst."

The shock shattered my thoughts into odd shapes and fragments. *Maybe I'll stay in this cabin, under the floorboards, but I won't live here.*

A Rescue

YOU WOULD NEVER HAVE KNOWN how depressed Patricia was, by the way she looked and the smile she wore like a mask. People described her as elegant. Patricia liked to joke that she made depression look good. She wore bright berry lipstick, a stylish gray coat, a knee-length skirt and cutesy flats with pink flowers when she walked her dog, a rescue. Her hair was perfectly styled, blow dried. On one side of her shoulders, her blond hair curled under, on the other side her hair curled over, but Patricia had learned to accept a certain degree of imperfection, or at least she was trying to. She never cried.

Every morning, she'd set an alarm, get ready and off they'd go. She had to get out of bed for Marvin. Patricia looked at the trees on her walk, their sprawling limbs reaching for a nonexistent sun, and tried to admire the asymmetry in nature, the beauty of it. It was something she had learned in therapy.

Breathe, she told herself. Breathe. The lake was foggy that morning. The air was moist in her lungs. She imagined leaping through the fog into the water, imagined swimming until she couldn't swim anymore, sinking, the gray water filling her lungs. Her heavy clothes dragging her down. Patricia staggered to a splintered wooden bench, in a haze.

Marvin, her floppy eared boxer, lab mix sat next to her. He cocked his head to the side, and watched her as she paused looking out at the gray that had absconded with the lake. The gray that was stealing everything. Some people loved fog, but not Patricia. It was claustrophobic. The world was shrinking. She was forgetting everyone she ever loved. They were disappearing into the gray.

She unclicked his leash and dropped it into the grass. "Go," she said.

No, Marvin seemed to say. He put his head on her lap, pushed his muzzle under her hand, nuzzling her fingers with his wet noise. *I'm here*, he told her. *I'm here. You aren't alone.*

She could hear him speaking to her, with his eyes, his little dog eyelashes and eyebrows shifting back and forth with concern.

Patricia wished she could climb some kind of ladder into the sky, above the trees, with their twisted black limbs, above the fog. Breathe unpolluted air. But she couldn't.

Marvin stayed at her side. He touched the back of her hand with his paw, in a slight, raking motion, but not hard enough to leave scratch marks.

I'm not leaving you, he seemed to say.

"Go," she said. "Dumb dog."

"You're going to find a better owner, a better family, run free. Go."

No.

"Well, fine then. I'm going now," she said. "You stay. Stay, Marv."

Marv sat still as she walked the limestone rocks and slipped off her gray coat and then her flats with the pink flowers. Her feet felt the rough stone, the odd, wet shapes, and she dropped them over the side, then slid in. The water was shockingly cold, even for summer. Maybe fifty degrees. Her teeth chattered. She looked back at Marv, his head cocked to the side, in a question, and she started swimming away. Her arms in front of her, in a slow breaststroke.

He was disappearing behind her into the gray. She felt a relief, a numbness, cold and floating… The land was gone. The pain was receding. There was only gray and water and a small circle of the world left in her vision. Pretty soon there wouldn't even be that.

But then, could she really do this to her dog? For a moment, she treaded water. What if no one wanted Marv? What if he languished in a shelter or was euthanized? She wondered if she should swim back, but which way was the land? Everything had disappeared in the fog.

And then she heard the splash. She twisted in the water and saw the little head bobbing behind her, ears flopping, entering her circle of vision.

"What part of stay do you not understand?" she scolded. "Go back, dumb dog."

I'm not going back. He doggie paddled steadfastly in her direction, and she swam away faster.

She felt his mouth tug at the back of her collar, felt him pulling her back to shore. At first, Patricia flailed, but he continued to tug at the back of her shirt, jerking her in the water. She gulped in and sputtered out. The water was cleaner than she expected, but she spat it out.

"Okay, okay," she said. "I got it from here. You can let go."

Patricia pulled herself up on the rocks, tripped, then caught herself on the limestone. Marvin scrambled up, shaking water off his coat.

He cocked his head to the side, and wagged his tail hesitantly. *I need you. Don't go.*

She picked up and put on her gray coat and her flats and threw her arms around him, and for the first time, ever, she wept.

"Marv, you dumb, disobedient dog. Nobody needs me."

I need you.

I'm not leaving you, he seemed to say.

Exhausted, Patricia lay down on the bench, shivering and wet, thankful the coat was dry, at least. The skirt clung to her thighs.

"Watch over me," she said. "I'm so tired. I'm so tired of everything. You have no idea. You don't understand, Marv. You don't understand what it's like to be human. You can't fix me, Marv. I'm broken."

I don't care that you are broken. I love you anyway.

She dozed off. She dreamt of the ladder out of the fog. Dreamt of climbing the rungs into the sunlight. And when she woke, the sun had burnt the fog off the lake, and a gentle breeze caressed her hair. The water reflected blue sky now. She felt the same as before, but less alone.

Patricia looked around for the leash, panicking that it wasn't in her hands when she awoke but Marvin was sleeping under the bench. He stood up slowly and stretched. Life wasn't perfect. It would never be. But *he* would never leave her.

Hey Charming

ONCE THERE WAS A FROG who turned into a man.

His skin felt so very dry, and the little hairs stood up on his arms. He shook cold and naked.

He craved flies, but his tongue lolled about in his mouth, short, fat and useless for catching prey.

Police thought he was a pervert because he was running around naked. Sirens wailed in the distance, painfully loud. As a frog, it never occurred to him to wear clothes.

Luckily, he was fast in his new body, dashing into the woods. He shielded his face with his arms as branches slashed by, whipping his bare legs.

And women walking in the forest kept mistaking him for a prince. Oh my.

He did have excellent abs.

The maidens followed him wherever he went, cat-calling out, "Hey Charming, rescue me please."

"I don't even know how to rescue myself," he yelled back. Bewildered.

He wasn't sure how he understood them, because human language was new to him. Maybe it was all part of the enchantment?

All he wanted was to go back to his pond and swim away, and so he did.

But his arms and legs weren't used to frog strokes.

What had once felt like flying through water, now felt like flailing and drowning.

A woman offered him a robe and towel at the water's edge.

He hated the gritty feeling of sand between stubby human toes.

Taking the robe, he discovered the warmth of fuzzy terry cloth drying his gooseflesh.

He sought out the witch deep in the forest, his delicate human feet cut on stones and twigs.

"Please … change … me … back, please," he begged in halting words.

"You did this to yourself," she said.

"What do you mean?" he asked. "I never asked for this."

"But you did," she said. "Under a full moon, you wished for a better life. Under a shooting star, too."

"You call this a better life? I want to go back to the way things were," he said. "I want to breathe underwater. I want to hop from stone to stone."

"You can't go back, only forward. You can only go one way. From who you were to who you are and then to who you will be."

And so the man who was once a frog moved into the swamp and became a hermit, hiding from the women, holed away in a little hut at the water's edge.

Sometimes, he hopped awkwardly over a makeshift bridge of stones, yelling at children collecting tadpoles in the water.

"Don't hurt them. Let them go. I was once a tadpole, too. I've changed many, many times. You'll change too."

But they never believe him. They never do.

A Killer Monologue, With Conviction.

OFFICER, I KNOW IT LOOKS BAD. Me standing here near where her body was found, drinking whiskey, but I swear to god I didn't kill her.

I never took Becca's body out in a little boat. I never put her remains in a plastic garbage bag and loaded her into a rowboat. I never paddled her out to the middle of the lake, I never tied her to bricks, at the waist. I never watched the black plastic puff and then sink.

I never removed her gold rings, Officer. I didn't keep them as souvenirs. I never kept a lock of her reddish-brown hair. I didn't hide them.

I wasn't the one who had been upset she was pregnant. I wanted that kid in my life.

I never hit her. But I watched the purple, blue bruises blossom on her arms like flowers days after when I saw her in secret. I never told her it was her fault. I always told her she was special, that she mattered, that she was a good person and she didn't deserve this.

You see, Becca was one of my best friends. Becca was my little sister. My parents used to send us to the park and told me it was my job to protect her. One time, on the merry-go-round, she fell and scraped her knee and I was the one who cried, and she told me, "Joshua, it will be okay." She was always telling me that. I felt so bad. I would never hurt her. You don't believe me, do you?

How do I know all these things about her death? My brother-in-law. Her killer. I'd tell you to talk to him. But I've already killed him. He confessed before I stabbed him.

And yes, I know it looks bad, Officer. And yes, I know I should have called a lawyer and I shouldn't be drinking, but I'm in shock. I'm in shock. And he got a few good punches in before I killed him. He hit me with a rock in the head quite a few times. I'm still bleeding—should really go to the hospital. You'll find his body in the lake, too, officer. Because I know that even though he was a sick bastard, she loved him, and she would have wanted to be with him. And it was the least I could do for her. But the asshole couldn't even do that for her. The asshole wouldn't sink.

Praying Porcelain

WHEN IT STARTED RAINING INSIDE Cynthia's room, she thought the roof had finally gone bad. It wasn't that outlandish of a scenario. After all, the roof was past its prime by about thirty-nine years. She and the house were "built" the same year and her parents had never replaced the roof, despite all the storms. The rain was everywhere, inside her blanket, soggy wet, cold against her skin. Her skin was chilled to the touch, gooseflesh had broken out on her arms and legs.

She had inherited the house from her parents and other stuff. Going through and packing up the boxes at first had seemed daunting. The dust collectors with their layers of gray, greasy fuzz. Small porcelain, praying figurines she pried from shelves, as if affixed by residual bacon grease. She had just thrown some of them out yesterday. No one wanted such things anymore, and she wasn't one for praying porcelain. She had stared at the little face, its little eyes were closed and eyelashes were painted on in blue. Maybe this was some kind of punishment from her parents for throwing it out.

She stood on her bed and reached up toward the ceiling. Running her hands on the surface, but she couldn't feel any bubble of paint or peeling drywall. She wanted to run and grab buckets, but didn't have any so she lined the floor with towels instead.

It didn't help.

The towels became saturated and things suddenly floated across the floor of the room, the carpet, like soggy moss beneath her bare feet. Boxes lifted off the ground.

Just what have I inherited? She wondered. Am I losing my mind? Are their ghosts punishing me, somehow able to control the weather? What kind of meteorological phenomenon was this?

It was up to her ankles, then her knees. The ice-cold water engulfed her legs. It reminded her of being in the ocean, of taking that first dive in. She tried to open the door, but it wouldn't budge. She went for the window. Hit it with her fists. Painted shut. "Goddamn it," she said, then felt her face flush. If they were ghosts, then they might not like her taking the lord's name in vain.

She looked out the window, pressed her face against it, and felt suddenly ill when she realized.

It wasn't even raining.

The sun was belting out a song outside.

"I must be dreaming. I've got to be dreaming," she said.

But she wasn't dreaming. It's hard to dream when you can't sleep.

The glass cracked. Cynthia wasn't sure if it was the pressure of her fists or the pressure of the water. It had reached her neck now.

"Dear God, what am I going to do?" she said.

"Oh, so *you're* praying now," a small voice said behind her.

The porcelain doll she had thrown out was on the tallest shelf in the room. The little blue painted eyelashes had shifted and its little eyes were now open.

In Case of Loss

"YOU CALL YOURSELF A GENIUS, but you can't remember your password?" Heather fumed. "You call yourself a genius." She muttered.

Steven flushed red and fiddled with his wedding band. He wanted to fling it at her, but his fingers were swollen and the band wouldn't come off. They were stuck together.

"Well at least I had the foresight to invest."

"Lot of good it does when you can't remember your password. Over $25.7 million-dollars in cryptocurrency is at stake, Steven, and you can't remember your password. Unbelievable."

"I wrote it down," he said. "I just need to find the notebook."

"Why can't you just remember the password, Steven?"

"I wrote it down so I wouldn't have to."

He didn't like the way she called him by his name. There was a time when she would have called him baby or a time when he would have called her darling. Now they were Steven and Heather respectively.

The small, black notebook had the password to his digital wallet. Unfortunately, he couldn't remember where he had placed it. He only had one try left on the password, before he was locked out of the account and the money was gone forever. The password eluded him. He went through the list of his pet names, had he added a question mark? A dollar sign, ampersand or a star? He'd never know. The time for guessing was over.

The laptop was shut in front of him.

Steven could remember the notebook. It was one of those little leather notebooks with rounded corners. He had bought it at a bookstore, a book temple. It was one of thousands he'd purchased over the years. At the time, it had felt satisfying in his hands, oddly real.

He wrote in them, poems, song lyrics. Strange lines, like "your eyes are a prison" and other nonsense. He wrote about Heather and other loves. More about destruction. Steven even wrote a plan to take over the world once. Steven styled himself a genius, but he was the kind of genius who could not remember his passwords, so maybe not much of a genius at all, he thought, rubbing his temples. He wasn't the kind of man who could hold a traditional job. It was one venture after another. And Heather loved him while the money was good but not when the money disappeared, or so he thought, and now the money was disappearing, literally with a small, black book.

"Have you seen my notebook?" he asked.

"What did it look like?"

"Well, it's small and black." He made a small rectangle with his hands to show the dimensions.

"Well, that narrows it down." She glared at him.

"What's it to you, anyway?" he asked. "It's my money. You are always running up our credit cards. If it weren't for you, Heather, we wouldn't be at risk of losing the house."

"It's our money," she said. "Half is mine. Steven, I've put up with so much. Don't get me started. And you are the one who forgets to pay bills, genius that you are."

He closed his eyes. He wasn't the easiest man to love, he knew that, too.

"This isn't helping." He sighed. "It's most likely on this shelf," he said. "I bet you or one of the cleaning crew put it up there with all the others."

The shelf of books behind him included hundreds of small journals.

"You aren't guiltless, you know," Steven said. "You haven't been the easiest partner."

Heather stood on a chair and started pulling them off the shelf and tossing the small notebooks to the floor, the pages fluttered on the way down, like birds.

"Do we have to do this fight now? I don't even know what I'm looking for," she said in a growl.

He was immersed in panic. He imagined dying. His heart pounded. He imagined clutching his chest and her calling an ambulance. He imagined her riding with him to the hospital. Begging him to tell her the password, to remember one last time. He was a man of imagination. And then he took another breath.

He imagined her looking through every black book, trying to decipher which word was his password. What was poetry. What was prose. What was what. And he smiled. She'd never figure it out. This both pleased and horrified him. The idea of her going through his writings.

"I can't even read your handwriting." Heather scowled. "You write like a crazy person."

"Don't call me that. You know I don't like that. And we need to be methodical," he said, trying to corral the wild, black books into stacks.

"Organization has never been your strong suit," she said.

"That's one thing I've always liked about you," he said. "You've got that and I don't. Can't we just work together on this one thing? If we can come together on this one thing, maybe everything will be okay. Let's have some wine and go through them together." He patted the stack of journals.

They opened a bottle, a cheap one. Still saving the others. He knew the password was on one of the first few pages, but he didn't tell her that. He flipped through stacks and stacks of the little black books. But it wasn't there.

"Let me check the nightstand," Heather said.

She came back with a little book and a smug smile.

"What would you do without me?" she asked.

He wondered for a moment. What would he do without Heather? They were a mismatched pair, like mismatched socks, he thought. One purple with polka dots and the other with green stripes. They were so wrong for each other, but also oddly comfortable, like a bad habit.

He opened to the first page. In case of loss, was printed there, along with the words return to and their old address from many years before.

And there on the first page was the password. The password was so stupid, he rolled his eyes. How could he forget it?

It was her name and their anniversary date. He had been that stupidly in love with her at that time. And now it was a date he could barely recall. He tried to remember the things he loved about Heather. He tried to remember that day, the day they were married, the way she looked at him. They didn't have much back then. She didn't care about the money then. Why did she care so much now?

"Did you find it?" she asked, peeking over his shoulder.

"No," I didn't." He swallowed.

She went quiet and so did he.

"Would you still love me if I had nothing?" he asked.

She paused. "Yes, I would."

"Where else could it be?" she asked.

"Can you check the bedroom closet?" He heaved a sigh.

She got up and went into the other room.

He put the notebook in his pocket, got up, put on his coat as quietly as he could. With his fingers on the doorknob, he looked over his shoulder and saw her at the other end of the hallway with tears in her eyes. For a moment, he wondered if she was going to ask him to stay.

"I helped you find it," she said, with gritted teeth.

He shut the door behind him, and he could still hear her yelling.

"And you call yourself a genius."

Lucky Shoes

I HAD A PAIR OF LUCKY SHOES. I found them on a body. Pried them off two warm, damp feet. The body was still alive. She was passed out and sleeping, slumped over on a bus stop bench on Hyde Park Boulevard. Her mascara streaked down and stained her cheeks, seemingly from sweat. Her steady breathing in and out smelled of booze.

The shoes were red satin, shimmery under a streetlight, slightly sensible, only an inch or an inch and a half high, those heels. I did not feel any remorse taking the shoes, because I left her my Nikes, and they were probably much more comfortable. I'm not actually heartless.

Luckily, the shoes didn't smell, as I took them off her feet. In fact, they smelled of lavender perfume.

Luckily, she was a size ten and so am I.

You could argue it was unlucky the approaching bus driver saw me crouched over her and called the cops, probably thinking I had done something to her.

I felt like I was flying, as a university cop yelled "Stop!" as his police car rolled down the street, next to me on the sidewalk. I couldn't stop laughing. It made it hard to breathe, but I sucked in air. His gun was drawn, but he didn't pull the trigger.

Luckily, the heels didn't snap, and the straps stayed on as I climbed the chain-link fence to get away half a block down. Heart pounding. Luckily, the cop didn't follow.

When I was free, I went dancing in those shoes, dancing in the alleys, dancing under yellow streetlamps all night. Dancing under the distant moon.

I didn't need the clubs. I didn't need the music. I didn't need a partner.

All I needed were my lucky shoes. Nothing hurt when I was wearing them. Not my heels, not my arches, not the balls of my feet, not my heart.

And finally, I sat down on a park bench and fell asleep at a different bus stop just as the sun rose. And when I woke, I wiggled my sweaty, naked toes with sadness in the daylight, but looked down and saw my Nikes on the ground. Waiting for me, beneath the bench. Lucky too.

Remembering the Future

I KEEP REMEMBERING THE FUTURE. I shout when I see you sleeping next to me. You are young, with dark stubble along your jaw and kitten breath. I barely recognize you with your smooth skin. In my mind, you are an old man, with gray whiskers, and a potbelly, and a cane from the accident. But here you are, slim, with muscular arms from playing basketball, the covers tucked underneath. In this time, I realize, we still play basketball in the hoop outside our building every day. I remember the sadness when that stopped, when you broke your spine in three places.

"What's wrong?" you mumble, as you open your eyes. They are blue again. No longer clouded by cataracts. For a moment, I wonder why you are not wearing glasses. You don't need them yet, do you?

"What year is it?" I ask.

"It's 2020," you say.

"One of the worst years," I say, with a groan.

"One of the worst years," you scoff. "It *is* the worst year ever."

"That's what you think," I say, shaking my head. "This is some of kind of weird dream," I say. "How is it thirty years ago? This must be some kind of mistake. I must have messed up. Why would I choose to come here?"

You stare back with a sleepy look.

"Why do I feel like my brain is scrambled?" I rub the sleep from my eyes. "I vaguely remember inventing a time machine, but it's a blur now. How did it work?"

"What are you talking about?" you ask gently. "Honey, did you take your medication last night?"

"Oh yes, my medication. Of course, I never miss my medication. But you can check the pill box, if you like."

You get up and look at the massive white and blue pill box and the plastic compartment slot for Tuesday p.m. is empty, of course, sitting next to the bathroom sink and an empty glass. "I don't mess around with my meds," I say.

You are wearing blue boxers, and I watch you walk across the room. You are slim and healthy. I am relatively slim and healthy. Funny, I remember at this age, thinking I was fat. I wasted my so many years wishing I was thinner or younger. At forty, you wish you were thirty. Silly. At fifty, you wish you were forty. Why can't you just enjoy your age and body? You learn the lesson too late, if at all. It's like finding a photograph and realizing what you couldn't see at the time.

I'm back in my young body. Only my mind has traveled. I remember the future. I remember a jumble of things that are to come. But the memories are fleeting. Temporary and fading. I know it gets worse before it gets better.

"Change of plans. Instead of going to the grocery store, I think we need to take you to see Dr. Miller," you say. "Just to be sure you are okay. We can stop at the grocery store to get some stuff on the way back."

You are afraid the meds have stopped working, but you don't say it out loud, because you don't want to worry me. I know you well enough to know this. I keep quiet.

We get into our Toyota Corolla. I strap on my seat belt. We listen to an old Coldplay song on the radio. "Paradise." It's an old song. I'm not sure why they are playing it. I remember thinking that before.

"Stop!" I yell, as you are about to turn left at the green light. "Don't go."

And at that moment, a Ford F150 barrels through the red light on the other side. The truck's engine roars by. My hand is on your chest, as though I could physically shield you from it. Your heart pounding so hard I can feel it.

"What the? How did you know?" you ask me. And I go pale and clench my hands together as though in prayer. It all flashes through my mind. I remember the broken glass. I remember the way your head danced sideways. I remember the sound of cracking and breaking and crunching metal. I remember blood and the wail of the ambulance. The cry of an animal that turned out to be me. The eerie quiet coming from you. Then the surgery. Helping you hobble around the house. I remember the second surgery. The third. The oval pain pills you took and what it took to get you off of them. And then it's gone. All in the flash of a speeding vehicle on the other side of an intersection. It's so simple, but it's not.

"I told you," I say. "I remember the future. You won't need the cane now."

I smile. I feel like I'm holding on to a fortune cookie future. That I know things, but they are vague. It's 2020, but I can feel 2021 in my fingers. 2022 in my toes. There's a muscle memory for 2023. You don't believe me. No one does. But every now and then when a flash comes back, I'll tell you something. You were always going to take me to the hospital this day. I remember.

You drive me to the hospital and sit with me in the emergency room. You visit me every day during visiting hours at the psychiatric ward, because you love me. And I'm not angry. Because I know you do. I remember. I know you will stay with me. I do not worry about you leaving because I am crazy. I have seen the future and you are there. There loving me. I remember decades of goodnight kisses on my lips.

A Botanical Affair

THE PLANTS HAD TAKEN OVER their apartment, since the pandemic started eight months before. Every week since it began, Mary's ex-lover, Quincy, a professor of botany, had sent one via FedEx. Some of them had lived and some of them had died shriveled deaths, but she couldn't seem to bear to throw them out.

The carcasses of ferns and lilies, and half-alive fiddle leaf fig intermingled with a lush trio of coconut palms. Some of them had names and some of them didn't. Wilson, Ferny and Mrs. Stubby. Lucy and Ethel from "I Love Lucy." Mary never gave up hope, even on the ones who seemed lost.

The Christmas cactus had stopped blooming. Something about the positioning of the windows, the orientation of the apartment. Perhaps it was the lack of southern light. The Christmas cactus had been Mary's favorite when it arrived. It was from the early days of the pandemic, when they were hopeful it wouldn't last so long and the plants didn't seem so strange.

She missed her meetings with Quincy from the old days. Her husband didn't. The plants had come between them. Physically and emotionally. A constant reminder of Quincy's presence in their lives. Quincy had a knack for growing animosity between them, not just plants.

"Do you miss him," Jeffrey asked her, as he leaned forward in his recliner and plucked dead blossoms off an African violet. "You really need to tell him to stop sending plants. I'm sure he's spending a small fortune, and this is ridiculous."

"I have," Mary said, peering out behind an overgrown, spindly fern. She was trying not to smile. "He said the idea was to cheer people up during tough times. That's noble, isn't it?"

"We should throw the plants away."

"We can't. They are living things. We can't just kill them. And just think about how much fresh air we are getting in the apartment. It's very healthy. Almost as good as being outside. The next best thing."

"Please give them away then," Jeffrey said. "For the love of all that is holy."

"Oh, Jeffrey," she said. "We really shouldn't come in contact with other people right now, and why can't you let me have them. They are beautiful. Why not let me have a little bit of joy? I've given up Quincy after all."

"And yet you hang onto his plants. You're having a botanical affair. I don't know why I tolerate this," he pushed a leaf back so he could get a better view of his wife. "I tolerate so much. Sixty-four potted plants of various sizes in a two-bedroom apartment. How much longer can we take this?"

"Do you really want us to move out in the middle of the pandemic and get a divorce right now?" she said. "It's not safe with Covid, looking at places. And I'd miss you honey. What's the point?"

"Maybe we should chance it," he muttered.

"I still love you, my dear," she said. "Don't you love me?"

He nodded.

"And besides," she said. "It's going to be a long winter. I wouldn't be surprised if there's another lockdown. A little greenery will do us good. Extra oxygen from the plants. How come you never send me any plants?"

"Mary, don't be ridiculous, we are drowning in plants. Where would you put them?"

"It's not that bad, is it?"

"Mary, this isn't healthy." He got up to pace the room and made it three steps before tripping on a burgundy rubber plant, and landing back on the couch.

"But the plants filter the air."

"Let him and his weird plants go."

"What kind of a man sends another man's wife a plant every week? It's like you've got the weirdest stalker with a green thumb ever."

"He's just an old friend who knows how much I love plants. I'm sure he sends everyone plants."

Just then the doorbell rang, and Mary expertly hopscotched over the pots to open it and find a six-foot-fall Chinese fan palm. She embraced the plant, pulling it inside the door.

"That's it," Jeffrey gritted his teeth. "I can't take it anymore. It's either me or the plants. Which do you choose?"

"You want me to toss out sixty-four plants?"

"Sixty-five now."

He leapt to his feet, and tripped on a prickly pear cactus, banging his head on the wall.

"Oh," Mary said, as he bled on the dried leaves of a monstera plant, "I'm beginning to see your point."

Jeffrey grabbed the Chinese fan palm and hurled it out the window pot-first. The breaking glass made a satisfying sound. The leaves fluttered through the air, as it sailed down, like an ineffective parachute. "There goes our deposit." Jeffrey sighed.

He placed a sheet over the window, but while they waited for the repair, the temperature plummeted inside the apartment. Almost all the plants were dead within hours. He grinned as he watched them turn brittle and brown.

"Murderer," Mary said, sniffling, as she surveyed the wilted, brown leaves and shivered. "This is so depressing, like a funeral of flowers."

"Don't worry," Jeffrey said with a shrug. "I'm sure we'll get another delivery next week. We can always start over. The pandemic's not over yet."

Stranger Across the Room

KELLY SEES HIM from across the restaurant. *But is it him? I'm imagining things*, she tells herself, and eats a bite of her linguine.

Kelly sees him. Or does she? If it *were* him, he'd be older than she remembers, just like this man. His hair has thinned, he's heavier, and his eyes look hazel. His mouth still has a pleasant way of turning up at the edges. He's smiling now at an older couple across from him. She can see the tops of their gray hair. The room is crowded.

Kelly tries not to stare, but she imagines he's staring back.

What are the chances? If it were him, they hadn't spoken in what? Fifteen years. Before her family existed. Just remembering brings chills, and her family seems to vanish next to her.

She clings to the conversation at her table. Her daughter is talking about a show she wants to watch. Kelly nods, but her husband asks about the rating. The girl mumbles, "twelve-plus," even though she's only nine. Her younger brother says, "ha, you're too young." She sticks out her tongue.

Of course, the man is staring. Because she's staring. Kelly looks down at her pasta. Absently twirls it with her fork. Remembering how it ended. Different jobs, different cities.

She'd cut off all contact, made the man a villain at the time. She'd had to. *His job had been more important than her.* Anger makes for a cleaner break.

He was not the love of her life. Her husband across the table was. A quiet man.

The kind you can sit with in comfortable silence. Her husband looks at her with a raised eyebrow, but doesn't press for an explanation. She doesn't say what she's thinking. Maybe later.

Is the man across the room a doppelganger? A ghost? Or the actual person? In a planet with billions of people, in the same restaurant?

Is the man perhaps offended that she hasn't said hello?

An imagination is a crazy thing. I need to lay off the wine. She puts down her chardonnay. *Or maybe I need to drink more.* More or less.

She squirms in her seat, remembering the way those eyes used to penetrate her.

He is still looking. She would never trade tables.

Her family is deep in a conversation about Minecraft, whether they should go fishing. She looks down at her husband's powerful hands on the table, the silver band on his fingers. Still shiny and mostly polished, despite a few scratches. More than a rebound.

Her husband makes her feel things no other man ever could, something more powerful than just ecstasy—Peace.

Connections can grow or be severed. The man at the other table is a handsome stranger, but they aren't connected.

Kelly takes another sip and looks over again. Wishing him happiness like hers.

When the man stands up to leave. His wife and baby are next to him in view now, along with a set of grandparents. Kelly smiles.

Is it actually him?

Strangely enough, that doesn't matter.

Catfishing in the Time of Covid

WHEN I WAS FIVE, I caught a catfish. When I was fifty, I was a catfish.

I toyed with a man named Marty on Facebook. A recent divorcee.

"Do you remember me?" I asked him on Messenger. "We used to be friends in fourth grade. You were my first crush."

Men always respond to flattery. I was pretending to be a woman named Susan. Usually, they go for the younger women, but sometimes I like a challenge.

Susan had somehow kept her figure. She was a sixty-year-old widow in her fake profile, of course. In real life, she was happily married with three grown boys. I get curious, so I know these things.

Susan had a long list of achievements in my version of reality. She was a retired RN and volunteered with Habitat for Humanity. There was a picture of her on a mission trip, surrounded by little, brown children, a picture with little hearts in the edges. Another of her holding a hammer and building a house. She had memes, so many memes. Religious memes to show what a good person she was. God is good. God is great. God is the answer. You could trust Susan.

"Do you remember Mrs. Flannigan?" Marty pinged me back on Messenger. "She was a great teacher. How I loved the sound of a sucker, the sound of a Messenger ding.

"Mrs. Flannigan had some good stories," I typed back.

"Yeah, she did," Marty wrote.

"I miss the playground," I said. "What's your life like now?"

"Well, with the pandemic, it's pretty lonely, to be honest."

"Wish I was there," I wrote back.

"Me too," Marty said. "Do you know the worst thing about this whole situation?"

"What?" I asked.

"The lack of human contact," he said. "I miss it."

"Me too." I shivered, pulling my blanket up over me as I lay in bed, with my laptop, the light glowing on my hands in the dark room with drawn blackout curtains. I had stopped bothering opening them. My studio apartment had started to feel like a prison. The big bed in the middle floated like an island in the middle of a shrinking sea. With the pandemic, my world was getting smaller every day.

"We could Zoom," he typed.

"I get Zoomed out," I wrote back. "But I could talk on the phone."

I gave Marty a number he could call, and we talked on the phone for hours. Even though he was ten years older than me, he had a warm, rich voice. Can you fall for your own victim? What if he was another catfish? That seemed unimaginable. There was something honest and kind about him.

Now I wondered if I could love him, if I had met him in real life under normal circumstances. I looked at his pictures, and wondered what he smelled like. I looked at the tousled, black hair, streaked with gray, and the deep, brown eyes. I wondered what it would be like to gaze into them. He had a serious look to him. In a strange way, Marty made my world feel bigger.

"Do you think we should meet sometime?" The idea terrified me, and not just because he'd find me out. It terrified me the way the possibility of love terrifies any sane person.

"Oh Marty," I said softly. "You know, it's not a good idea right now. We live in different cities. Travel isn't safe at the moment, and I've been thinking of coming out of my early retirement and helping out at the hospital."

"I know," he said. "I meant one day."

"One day, yes."

The lies spilled out of my mouth so easily. I had a talent for them and I hated myself for each one I told. I hated myself for each and every one. I knew I had to ask him for money soon. Money. That's what this was about, right? Not my own profound loneliness. Not trying to fill it.

I found myself looking forward to his calls. We talked every evening for hours. We often talked about mundane things like the weather. "I have trouble sleeping," I told him. "I wake up in the middle of the night and I can't fall back asleep."

"That's pandemic stress for you," he said. "I feel that too."

In the afternoon, he'd tell me about the clouds above his house or the birds in his yard out in the country. He had books that named them. We never talked about Covid or our supposedly shared hometown. We talked about dreams and what they meant.

"What's your vision for 2021?" he asked. "Assuming you're vaccinated?"

"I want to travel," I told him. "I want to see the world. I want to go to France and write a book in the countryside." I don't know why I told him the truth that day, but then again, it wasn't the first time.

After all these months alone in the dark room, I wondered what it would be like if Marty were there with me in that bed, with his arms around me. What it would feel like to be held, to feel Marty's lips pressed against my hair, his chest against my face. I laughed out loud, a bitter laugh. "Marty, do you think we will ever find love again?" I asked him during one of our calls.

"We have to have faith," he said. "That things will get better. And we have to learn to see the love that we already have."

I stood up and opened the curtains. I looked out at the street below, at the birds flitting back and forth on the street.

"How do you tell the difference between a sparrow and a swallow? Is there a difference?" I asked him.

"Does it really matter?" he had said.

I wondered if there was that much of a difference between Susan and me. A swallow and a sparrow. Of course, there was.

As he listed off details I quickly forgot, I realized I had earned enough of his trust, and that I had told him too much. Some of the stories were real and mine. I'd told him about the bicycle accident I'd had when I was nine. I'd pedaled down a steep, grass-covered hill as fast as I could and hit a hole in the ground at the bottom. I flew through the air, and when I landed, I was completely fine. Until the bike fell on top of me, giving me a bloody nose. I felt kind of like that now.

I stopped contacting him for a few days. Enough days that he started to worry. That he sent messages asking if I was okay. "I pray you're all right," he wrote.

I lay in bed, not eating, not sleeping, shivering, neither ill or well. Knowing that I was a horrible person. Wishing I could call him and tell him how awful I was, confess all my sins.

Instead, finally, I sent the message saying I had gotten in trouble, that I needed money for bail. I asked for a wire transfer. The nice thing about catfishing is you can work from home. It's convenient during a pandemic. The bad thing about it having to say goodbye and the psychological toll that entails. It's a specific skill set. You've either got it or you don't. I was losing it. I knew it was time for a new career. Time for a change. I was surprised when the wire transfer came through. To this day, I don't really understand why he did it.

Marty sent twenty grand along with a message:

To whoever you are, I sincerely hope you enjoy writing in France. Take care and God bless.
–Marty.

P.S. My fourth grade teacher's name was Mrs. Johnson, not Mrs. Flannigan.

Barbara, the Bank Robber

ROBBING A BANK during a pandemic is easy. No one thinks twice when you show up in a mask, wearing rubber gloves. Add sunglasses, and really, you could be anybody. Barbara had always wanted to rob a bank, and she was dying of kidney failure, anyway. She wanted to leave something for her eleven grandchildren other than outrageous medical bills. A legacy. A legend? Maybe, but who would believe it?

She got the idea while she was hooked up to a dialysis machine with the tubes of blood going in and out of her body. She chuckled, thinking about minimizing the dangers of coronavirus vs bullets from an armed security guard. Her children wouldn't let her go to the grocery store, the library, the mall, anywhere really. What kind of life was this, anyway? A life afraid of death. Even though it was coming. Even though the days were fleeting. She couldn't see them except on

Zoom or Facetime, and it wasn't enough. The only trips out were to the dialysis clinic three times a week. The doctors estimated she might have another year at best. She couldn't afford to wait to live.

Barbara smiled, imagined her children finding her dead in her bed, and the cash from the robbery waiting for them in her desk drawers, piles and piles of it. She'd have to make it easy to find so they wouldn't overlook it. Or maybe she'd whisper in her daughter's ear about the fortune that awaited the family with her last breaths. What would she say? Honey, there's a lot of money in my mattress? What if she couldn't tell her and the mattress was sold or donated?

Four hours on a dialysis machine at a time provided plenty of time to plan a heist and think these things through. She'd even hide her gender. Taped what was left of her breasts, wore men's clothing, an old flannel shirt and a pair of baggy jeans. Nikes. Practiced dropping her voice an octave. "Give me the money," she'd say in front of the mirror, wearing her mask, the cloth muffling her voice. "Empty the vaults. Push the alarm button, and I'll kill you."

She had no intention of killing anyone. It was a dream really. The pandemic had made her that bored, that stir crazy.

And they kept the lobby open for some inexplicable reason during the pandemic, which made it easier. Stupid, greedy bank execs.

First step was stealing a car. Not that hard. Barbara watched a series of YouTube videos on the easiest to steal models and chose an inconspicuous vehicle, a GMC pickup. She felt powerful, rumbling through the intersections, bouncing slightly in her seat.

When she got out of the pickup, she got out slowly down to the ground. She had to be careful with her low blood pressure and not get light-headed. Barbara took a cautious step over the uneven, raised doorstep, entered the bank and slowly walked up to the window. There was a flimsy plastic barrier between her and the teller.

She brandished her gun. "Give me $10,000, now!" she demanded. "Pack it up fast."

The blood drained from the teller's face. The woman couldn't have been older than her eldest granddaughter. Maybe twenty-four. "No problem," she said, softly. "But I'll have to go to the back to get that kind of cash."

"You push an alarm, I start shooting people," Barbara said in a deep voice. "You hear me?" While on dialysis, she'd decided if she had to shoot someone, she'd go for the less fatal body parts, a toe rather than a head, for example. She smiled under her KN95 mask.

"No problem." The woman packed up the bills. "What denomination would you like them in?" she asked.

"Twenties," Barbara said. "Hurry up, now." She threw a crumpled tote bag at the teller. "Fill it up quick."

"I've got a son," the teller said softly. "He's thirteen months old. He just started talking, called me Mama yesterday for the first time." Her voice trembled as she spoke.

"I don't want to hear it," Barbara said, clenching her jaw under the mask. Under normal circumstances, she would have asked to see a picture. But nothing about this year was normal.

When the bag was full, she walked out, with it, swinging it under her arm. A pang of disappointment that it was too easy.

She swung open the door, stepped out into the sun, and that's when she tripped on the uneven, raised doorstep. The tote bag full of money went flying, the twenties fluttered past her in a cloud in a gust of wind. It was like being a contestant in a game show gone horribly wrong. A stream of money gushed past her.

Barbara tried to get up but couldn't, something was broken. A rib, maybe her hip too. The pain was sharp. The teller was talking to someone. "They'll be here any minute. Don't worry."

The gun was still in Barbara's hand. Would she make good on her promise to shoot if they sounded an alarm? Of course not. There were no bullets in the chamber, which was lucky. Otherwise, it might have gone off.

But don't feel too bad for her. Barbara did not succeed in robbing the bank, but she did successfully get money for her daughter. No one believed an eighty-two-year-old woman in her right mind was capable of robbing a bank. They all thought she was going senile. And the lawyers argued that she didn't have much time left. The robbery failed, but the lawsuit over the uneven doorstep did not.

Arnav and the Apocalypse

I NEVER EXPECTED TO LOVE ARNAV, and I certainly didn't intend to have his baby at a time like this.

When the journalists first told us the zombie apocalypse had begun, I didn't believe them. No one did. The president came on TV and said it was just like the flu and it would go away in the first few months. But the second wave of the undead was worse than the first.

It was a day to remember, actually impossible to forget. My neighbor Amelia had become infected. She waved at me as I was mowing my lawn with the manual push mower—her arm was purple and bloated. I wasn't worried that she was going to jump the fence, and not just because of the barbed wire that Arnav had wound up on the top. She wasn't an agile woman. Amelia was large in life, and large in un-death. Her rotting ligaments never could have made that leap to eat my brains.

Arnav ran out to me in his pajamas, in his flip-flops. "Silly honey," he said. "You shouldn't be mowing the lawn in your condition."

"I need the exercise, and what condition?" I asked blankly.

"Haven't you noticed? I'm pretty sure you're pregnant," he said.

Arnav had noticed the nausea, and the extra restlessness before I did. He noticed the strange cravings. I had wanted Korean food so badly the night before. I frowned. Maybe this is why he had risked his life to get me kimchi and confirmed just how bad it had gotten downtown.

He had wandered through the hordes of zombies in his trusty Honda Civic. "To pick up provisions" at the Korean grocery store. And kimchi because I hadn't been able to stop talking about how much I missed kimchi.

I never deserved Arnav. We'd been roommates for seven months, and he was a good guy. It was quite convenient we fell in love, because it wasn't time to be on Tinder. You never knew if your date would be infected or not, if his arm would fall off. Or more importantly, his member.

Arnav was thoughtful and intelligent. Beautiful too. Tall, slender. Intense, with dark eyes, and golden skin. He could name all the capitals. You could quiz him on them, and he took pride in that. "What's the capital of Liberia," I asked him in bed once, and he'd shouted back, "Monrovia" with a little too much enthusiasm that night.

"You're such a dork," I said, lying next to him in bed, my face against his chest.

He thwacked me with the pillow. I laughed, and he climbed on top of me.

My love for him snuck up on me. I never expected it. At first, we'd been worried about religious differences, but he prayed to his gods arranged on the kitchen counter with little, brass oil lamps, and

I prayed to my God on my knees by the bed, and it didn't seem to matter because the world was ending. We were hedging our bets. Arnav was a man of many hyphens and nationalities sandwiched together. Canadian-Indian-American. Sometimes, we talked about fleeing to another country as refugees, but we weren't sure it was better anywhere else.

He was handy during an apocalypse. Arnav had stocked up on bags of rice and dals in the beginning and seeds to grow in our garden. His paranoia paid off. His chili pepper plant was his pride and joy and was high in vitamin C.

"We're going to be okay," he said. "We can ride through this for years."

At first, I hadn't wanted to complicate things, but Arnav promised me he wouldn't let our romantic status destroy our ability to be good to one another.

"I will always respect you. I will always be good to you. I'll never hurt you. I promise." The words sounded almost like wedding vows. They sent a chill through me.

"It's a tough time to make promises," I said. "But thank you." Inwardly, I had cringed at not promising anything back. Even though it was early days, the apocalypse had already taught me not to make promises I couldn't keep, so I didn't. I didn't make any.

Sometimes I thought Arnav knew how to read my mind. I'd shiver, and he'd bring me a sweater. I'd sigh, and he'd give me a hug.

He read the news every day on his phone, spending hours doom-scrolling. Most of the journalists were dead by then, and there were just rumors on Twitter and random videos, many made up by old Russian bots and conspiracy theorists. No one wanted to believe it was the end of the world, but it was.

"I'll read it for you," he said. "It affects you too much."

It's strange the things you learn in an apocalypse. I've learned to pay attention only when needed. I've learned how to roast squirrel and rabbit, and crochet and sew. I've learned how to grow vegetables and barter, how to spot an infected person by the way they smell. I've learned to live without tea—probably better for the baby anyway.

And Arnav. Arnav who could read my mind like he could read the news. Arnav who knew I had his baby growing within me before I did. Arnav who had these beautiful brown eyes. I'm telling you I loved him, and I tried not to notice the scent over the smell of the grass.

Because it was not just the neighbor. That kimchi craving cost me. Cost us.

I knew when I got back in the house something had to be done. Arnav knew too.

"Honey. I promised you I'd never hurt you," he said sweetly. "You do what you need to do." He pulled out the gun from the kitchen cupboard and put it on the table with a box of bullets.

"You already know, I didn't just pick up kimchi last night at the Korean grocery store," he said. "It was bad out there. I didn't want to tell you everything last night. I knew you'd have a hard time sleeping, and I just couldn't find the words."

I started to sob, and I couldn't speak through the shaking of my chest.

"Don't feel guilty, honey. Don't cry. You know we needed those provisions. For the baby, too. I'm sorry, sweet honey."

He kissed me sweetly on the cheek, opened the box of bullets and loaded the chamber of the gun. "We've got a few decisions to make," he said. "Before the infection takes hold."

"Cognitive decline is one of the first symptoms," I mumbled, more to myself then him.

"Keep asking me my capitals," Arnav said. "You'll know when I start slipping."

"I don't know the right answers anyway," I held back another sob, tried to stop the shaking of my body. "Geography was never my strong suit in school. It's just not emphasized in the States. Our maps were so outdated in school."

"You'll know if I got it wrong," he said. "I should probably shoot myself outside, so it's less messy, and you can burn my body. My parents would be pleased with the cremation, and it's less of a risk that I'll rise."

I couldn't stop the tears from rolling. "Arnav. You can't shoot yourself. You'll go to hell," I said.

"Silly honey," he said. "Your God will understand, trust me. And I don't believe in your hell."

"I'll shoot you," I said, picking up the gun with trembling hands. "Just in case."

"But wouldn't that make you a murderer?" Arnav raised an eyebrow at me.

"It's an act of self-defense," I said. "Even if I don't wait for you to become a monster."

"I don't want you to remember me that way," Arnav said, folding his arms.

"I'll always remember you as you," I said simply.

"Arnav," I said.

"Yes," he said.

"What's the capital of Madagascar?"

"Antananarivo." The name rolled off his tongue impossibly. He smiled broadly.

"Is that right?" I asked.

"Yes," he said.

"My goodness," I said. "I can't believe I'm going to have to raise a baby on my own in the middle of a zombie apocalypse…"

"I'm sorry."

"It's not your fault," I said.

"Um, yeah it is."

"Let's not talk about that now. We don't have a lot of time. I was thinking, maybe I should name our baby after you," I said, swallowing.

I wanted to ponder whether the child would look like Arnav or me. I wished I could call my parents with the news, but they didn't make it past the first wave. I didn't care that we weren't officially married at this point. I just wanted some semblance of joy. But the scent. That smell. The joy was stolen from us already. I wanted to throw up from panic and grief.

"Where did they get you?" I asked.

"On my right thigh." He pulled down his pajama pants and showed me the gash. It was oozing yellow, green and purple pus already. A bad sign that made me queasy. Arnav swallowed. I know he was trying to be brave.

"We'd better make preparations," he said.

"Arnav, I don't know if I can raise a child alone," I said, the fear rising in my voice. "Under these conditions."

"Honey, you've got a lot of food, you've got firewood. You've got water. You've got plenty of bullets and excellent aim."

"Not exactly, the items I thought I'd need on a baby registry. What about diapers? A crib."

"A dresser drawer can be used as a bassinet, if you pull it out. Promise me, you'll give it a shot," he said. "The whole survival thing. As long as you can. I know you'll figure it out. You're resourceful and amazing."

"I can't believe you are leaving me here, in this situation." I cried.

"I'm sorry I put you in this position alone. I messed up."

He stepped back into his pajama pants, held me in his arms, and kissed my hair. I could smell the rot on him, mixed with his familiar scent.

"You've been the love of my life," I said.

"We were lucky to have this time together," Arnav said. "I've been so lucky." He swallowed.

"What's the capital of Tanzania?"

He hesitated for a moment, his eyelids fluttering strangely, then said, "Dodoma."

"Is that right?" I asked. I wondered if my American education and lack of geographical knowledge would cost me my life. Or if I cared. But then again, I had to think of the baby now. A mix of excitement and dread filled my belly. I shouldn't want this baby, but it was all I had left. I *did* want him, her, whatever it was.

Arnav walked into the garage and carried some firewood out to the yard, and came back for the shovel and gasoline. I followed. He started digging a hole. I watched the sweat drip down his forehead, the muscles twitch and tremor erratically, seize the shovel awkwardly. He dug the hole, stopping and starting as if forgetting where he was and what he was doing. His eyelids fluttered, revealing the whites of his eyes.

I held the gun now. I should have also grabbed a sweater. I was shaking and trembling. Was it the cold or the adrenaline?

He was quiet now. I knew what I had to do.

"Arnav," I said.

"Yes… silly honey," he said slowly, pausing to wipe the sweat from his forehead. His beautiful brown eyes were back.

"What's the capital of Argentina?"

"La Paz," he said quietly, looking far away.

This time, I didn't have to ask him if he was right or wrong or whether I should pull the trigger. Arnav knew how to read me. And after all this time together, I knew how to read him. I didn't have to wait for him to drop the shovel and leap for me. I didn't have to wait for him to turn into something he never wanted to be. I aimed, and I closed my eyes so I wouldn't see, and he could have moved. Arnav could have flinched. He could have fled, but he didn't. He took the bullets because he loved me.

Five years have passed, Arnavi and I have picnics in the backyard on a blanket near where her father's cremains are buried, a mix of traditions, his and mine. Most of the houses around us have been looted and burned to the ground. Our bullets and seeds have come in handy. I have Arnav's old atlas in my lap, a prized possession I found in his things. I quiz my daughter about capitals. I've learned them too. It's a thread that connects her with the father she never met, and with a world she's never known. I can almost hear Arnav when I do, and I know what he'd say. I can almost hear him whispering now.

"Silly honey, why learn the names of cities that no longer exist?"

It's a question Arnavi sometimes asks, too.

ACKNOWLEDGMENTS

THERE AREN'T ENOUGH WORDS to acknowledge the people on my publishing journey.

A massive thank you to my amazing editor, Jennifer Bisbing. Thank you for challenging me to be a better writer and take artistic risks. You are a talented author and poet as well, and it's an honor working with you.

To Polly Letofsky and the My Word Publishing team. Thank you for your mentorship and inspiring me to really get my book out into the world.

Thank you to Graphic Designer Victoria Wolf for excellent interior design and being such a wonderful pro to work with. You inspire me with your art and writing, too. Much gratitude to Shira Atakpu of Shira Lee Designs for a cool cover that matches the spirit of the book.

To authors Kathy Fish and Nancy Stohlman, whose flash fiction retreat in Italy changed my life in numerous ways for the better. Thank you for your inspiration, friendship and kindness.

Thank you to my Chicago writing buddies, Indie City Writers, especially authors TaKaylla Gordon and M.L. Kennedy.

Thank you to my Colorado writing buddies, Catherine Spader, Camille Parker, Alexandra O'Connell, Mary Walewski and all the other talented folks who show up for our writing sessions on Zoom.

Thank you to the THC Story Contest, for recognizing my story, "Grandma" with a second place, $300 cash prize. Much gratitude to *Cherry Magazine* for publishing "Dark Angels," "Arsonist Housewife" and "Final Jeopardy." Thank you to the *Dapper Press Lounge* for publishing "Dark Angels," as well. Thank you to the ReedsyPrompts blog contest, for shortlisting and inspiring "Killer Blossoms."

Thank you to friends, Karen Yaeger, Matt Yaeger, Jen Kolic and Katie Kothenbeutel, for always cheering me on.

Thanks again to my husband, daughter, parents, siblings and family for all the love. Pandemics are hard on writers. But it's easier when you've got great people in your life.

ABOUT K.B. JENSEN

K.B. JENSEN is an award-winning author, with two novels, *Painting With Fire*, an artistic murder mystery, and *A Storm of Stories*, which veers literary. K.B. lives in Littleton, CO, with her family and rescue mutt. Her work has appeared in *Cherry Magazine*, *Progenitor* and other publications. She enjoys skiing and writing poetry. To find out more, visit www.kbjensenauthor.com. If you enjoyed, *Love and Other Monsters in the Dark*, please consider leaving an honest review on Amazon or Goodreads.

INVITE K.B. JENSEN TO YOUR BOOK CLUB

AS A SPECIAL GIFT TO READERS, K.B. would love to visit your book club in person or via Zoom. Please contact K.B. directly to schedule her appearance at your book club meeting. She can be reached at kbjensen.author@gmail.com.

OTHER BOOKS BY K.B. JENSEN

Painting With Fire: An Artistic Murder Mystery
A Storm of Stories